TOOTH & CLAW

TOOTH & CLAW

DAVE JEFFERY

A
Grinning Skull Press
Publication
PO Box 67, Bridgewater, MA 02324

Tooth & Claw

This book is a work of fiction. All characters depicted in this book are fictitious, and any resemblance to real persons — living or dead — is purely coincidental.

The Skull logo with stylized lettering was created for Grinning Skull Press by Dan Moran, http://dan-moran-art.com/.
Cover designed by Jeffrey Kosh, http://jeffreykosh.wix.com/jeffreykoshgraphics.

ISBN: 1-947227-31-9 (paperback)
ISBN-13: 978-1-947227-31-6 (paperback)
ISBN: 978-1-947227-32-3 (e-book)

DEDICATION

For Tom and Grace

CONTENTS

Acknowledgments

I wish to thank Mike and Harrison at Grinning Skull Press for taking on this little slice of lunar mayhem, and the editorial team for tightening the leash. Further thanks go to Gard Goldsmith, Tom Deady, Tony and Jim over at Ginger Nuts of Horror, and Thomas Joyce at This is Horror for their inspiration, encouragement and support. Finally, thank you to my readers for coming along for the ride. You're all amazing.

Prologue

He ran, earth-pounding, heart-pumping, and headlong. About him, the dense woodlands provided no respite; the monsters chasing him had the advantage, the die forever cast in their favor. He could hear them now in the distance, the whoops and screams of delight, the bloodlust making them confident and weakening his resolve.

How the hell had it come to this? Where had it all gone so wrong? He wasn't a bad person; he worked as a medic, for Christ's sake. A third of his thirty-five years on this earth had been devoted to caring for and saving the lives of others. In fact, his last memory was leaving St. Norman's General Hospital after a twelve-hour shift. He recalled heading to his car, a second-hand Honda Civic. Then someone had stepped from the shadows and every cell in his body wanted to explode as the crackle of a taser sliced through the air.

He'd woken god-knows-how-much-time later, dazed and caged. A monotone voice through the Tannoy system in the plasterboard ceiling had told him the deal. He'd be released from the cage. All he had to do to earn his freedom was evade capture. The question as to why he'd been chosen was always at the back of his mind, but survival instinct took charge as soon as he was blindfolded by two thickset security guards. They had ignored his pleas and questions, threatening instead that he would get the taser again if he didn't *shut the fuck up*.

He was dumped in woodlands, told to wait five minutes before removing the hood. It wasn't a request.

Now he was running for his life. No cliché, no adage, just total and utter fact. The terrain proved a treacherous obstacle of low branches cutting into his face and thorny bushes tearing at his clothing and the exposed flesh of his hands.

An embankment loomed ahead, the embodiment of his current dilemma. He went low, digging his hands into the undergrowth, using the foliage to drag his exhausted body to the brow, spurred on by the thought that he might actually find a way out.

There was a dull thud, and the ground next to his head exploded in a plume of dirt and leaves. He cried out in surprise, climbing to his feet, lurching, then falling forward to all fours, scampering up the incline like a proverbial scared rabbit.

There came another dull thud and a momentary sharp, searing pain in his lower back. His severed spinal cord took pity on him and robbed him of all feeling below his waist. His legs collapsed, and he rolled down the embankment, crashing through the bracken until he lay on the woodland floor. He watched the two men emerge from the nearby bushes, shouldering suppressed hunting rifles as they came. Their night vision goggles made them appear more inhuman than their actions.

There was resignation that his final moments were playing out. Confirmation came when one of the men pulled a serrated hunting knife from his belt, stooped, and cut his throat.

The two men watched their prey bleed out, life draining from his eyes.

"Man, don't you just *love* this fucking place?" the man with the knife said.

"Damn straight," his colleague replied with a grin.

His partner smeared blood from the knife across his own sweaty brow. He offered up the blade.

The other man shook his head. "Your kill, your honor."

"Okay, boss."

As one man sheathed the knife, the other pulled out his cell phone from his green windbreaker, activating it with a single touch of his thumb. The line kicked in, and he spoke with barely suppressed excitement.

"We're ready for the next one."

Chapter One

The spruce trees created a jagged edge to the skyline, above which the incoming chopper was a mere smudge against the gray clouds. The thick staccato of rotor blades rolled across the valley, and the landscape below wavered as foliage succumbed to the caress of the breeze coming in from the southwest.

The undulating countryside leveled off, giving way to a huge lawn, and perched on the edge of beautifully rich, manicured grass was Cofton Grange, its quarter turrets and yellowed sandstone still glimmering in the fading light.

The stately home was built in 1709 on the site of Brunswick Hall, an equally grand building that had become a victim of canon-fire in 1645, at the height of the English Civil War. Before its demolition, Brunswick Hall had a reputation for attracting controversial figures. There were rumors that several key members of the Gunpowder Plot had stayed in its halls during the original planning stages, and its spurious amity had extended to hosting a dinner for Matthew Hopkins, the notorious Witchfinder General when he passed through the lands.

When The Grange was built, it continued with its tradition of associations with the shadowy side of society. Highwayman Dick Turpin held up three coaches on nearby roads, and Sally Salisbury, a notorious celebrity prostitute, allegedly frequented parties before her imprisonment in 1723. During the first 100 years, The Grange had seen both the French and American revolutions, unprecedented stability of the Ottoman Empire, and the publication of *Gulliver's Travels* and *Robinson Crusoe*. For the locale, it was a constant entity, as was the twelve-hundred acres of hills and woodlands that made up its estate.

Another constant was the man who watched the inbound chopper with eyes the color of gray marble. Just like the grand building rising up behind him, Jacob Rothschild's refined exterior was a facade that hid an ugly and controversial past. He was mild-mannered and soft spoken. His eyes were cupped in heavy lids, and his cheeks were high and angular. Although he had a slight frame and fell two inches short of six feet, his presence commanded attention the way a head teacher's silent poise quells a hall of rowdy kids.

Albert Rothschild, Jacob's father, had also commanded authority. But his presentation—his means—of getting things done was perhaps not as refined, not as polished, as those adopted by his son in the years that were to come. That was not to say Jacob was averse to extreme prejudice; on occasion, it was a necessary part of his business. But his father used violence as a tool to send a very clear message to those reluctant to play ball. For Jacob, it was about keeping people *quiet.*

His father was an effective criminal but lacked vision. He didn't see anything beyond money and providing for his family. Jacob understood the perverse nobility of fatherhood and the responsibilities that came with such a role. The fact he had not sought to have a family was a testament to the belief that grand success and the shackles of family life simply did not mix. Either way, when his father was gunned down in a pub in Birmingham as he ate pie and cheese-mash, Jacob and his mother had to get savvy, and damn quick. When their crime empire appeared vulnerable, Jacob was twenty-one years old and had his own portfolio, underworld property (mainly safe houses for those on the run), and trafficking anything that could be crammed into cramped spaces. It was a modest business, but once he siphoned his father's assets into it and they got the hell out of town, the whole thing grew beyond profitable. By the time he'd acquired The Grange, his personal assets were estimated at over 1.5 billion.

All of it squeaky-clean.

At the point where he took on The Grange, the commercial and physical integrity of the estate was in dire straits: the building run down and the grounds neglected after being poorly managed by Lord Atwitch, a third-rate businessman with a bought title.

During the acquisition, Rothschild had agreed to be a silent partner to bring the house and grounds back to their former glory. But his motivation was not about gaining privilege or titles; it was about hiding in plain sight. Yes, the thought the house had a history of assumed notoriety did give it a whimsical attraction, but Rothschild was above all of that because there was no doubt from anyone who knew him that he was an exceptionally good criminal.

In the first eight years of renovating The Grange and its bank balance, he had taken over responsibility for Grange Holdings PLC, the company created with the intention of bringing the building back to its glory days. After ten years, the entire estate belonged to him, the previous owner having sold over the deeds shortly before "disappearing abroad." In truth, Lord and Lady Atwitch were strangled and dismembered while on holiday in the US before their carcasses became a special treat for the guests at an alligator farm in Louisiana. Just like the nefarious affairs of The Grange itself, this rumor had no evidence to support it.

Over the next twenty years, Rothschild and his mother turned The Grange into a prosperous and thriving estate, generating a place tourists and top-end pleasure seekers alike clamored to visit. And visit they did, in droves; business was thriving, with so many people and so much money changing hands.

But success was a cloak behind which the real industry thrived. And that industry was, of course, crime. Top-end, high-stakes crime.

Over time, Jacob had become as successful as he was secretive, and these two facets were intrinsic, a synergy that maintained his prestige. His mother had died only two years ago, in one of the rooms at The Grange, a team of care-givers making sure her end came with both comfort and dignity. It was the first and last time for many years Jacob could remember crying. Not in public, of course. At the funeral (she'd been interned in the family mausoleum deep in the woods), he'd been stoic and refined, the persona he wore as well as his suit. Later, in his chambers, he'd allowed the tears to fall.

He relished the grief, knowing that his long-suffering mother deserved every single tear he'd shed for her. Without this gentle and unassuming woman in his life, his primary focus had become his business interests.

Jacob's focus at that moment, however, was the H155 heading toward him. The helipad was twenty meters away, a raised concrete plinth with a short run of steps down to a wide gravel path. As well as the approaching chopper, he was also mindful of the events that had been planned for the coming evening. It was a special time for special people, exceptional people that operated beyond the realms of the humble commoner. Though he'd never admit it to anyone else, Jacob didn't think it was too conceited to consider the events laid out were even above kings and queens themselves.

Yes, some things could be bought with money. But not everything.

Nature had a price list all of its own.

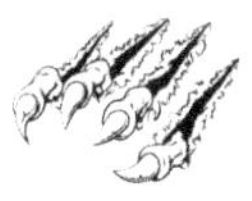

The helicopter made three trips and brought a guest list of four people. As each passenger disembarked, Jacob greeted them. Standing at his side was Sanders—a waiter dressed in a smart white tunic and starched black trousers—who carried a flute of iced champagne on a small, silver serving tray.

In his mid-thirties, Sanders had striking blue eyes and a neatly trimmed beard. He was immediately attentive to the guests as each disembarked, and he escorted them to their rooms on the third floor with a confident air.

As he walked, Sanders paid careful attention to each of them, his face scrutinizing every move, every nuance. Each of the guests considered this a sign of his time and expertise in service.

They could not have been more wrong.

In one of the guestrooms, Martin "Marty" Woodhead placed his travel bag on the edge of the huge four-poster bed. The headboard was made from Blackwood, carved with intricate two-dimensional images of peacocks with tail plumage extended like great, ornate fans.

Marty sat on the mattress as he took in the room, his feet bumping against the valance. The guest room was large, and the floors were covered in plush carpet and thick, expensive-looking rugs that were vibrant, as though they had been bought that very day. The walls, covered in heavy wallpaper, had garish patterns, and heavy drapes hung like burgundy sentinels to either side of the high, leaded windows. The furniture was old, each sideboard or small table warped and pitted by age, but the surfaces gleamed with lacquer and varnish. He sniffed and gave out a small sneeze, dust and the smell of wood heavy in the air.

He shuffled forward so that his backside was almost sliding off of the bed; only then could he plant his feet on the floor. He dug his heavy boots into the carpets, enjoying the way the pile gave way under his soles like he was walking through lush, green grass.

Marty sighed.

He was a small man with big issues. To anyone who ever asked the question, he'd say he had no truck with being five feet-four inches tall. Inside, however, his mind would play out how he could gleefully gut the inquisitor without thought. Instead, he would pull his bearded lips into a casual smile, his deep brown eyes twinkling with mischief.

Over the years, he'd compensated for his lack of stature but building up his physical prowess. He boasted a black belt in karate, could bench press two-hundred-and-fifteen pounds, and had completed three Iron Man challenges.

As he thought about what had brought him to The Grange that evening, he pawed at his foppish fringe, brushing strands of dirty gray-blond hair from his brow. It was a nervous trait he'd inherited from his mother. Over the years, she'd used it as a ploy to distract his moronic father from doling out another beating to Marty for being "so fucking weak."

Ultimately, the bruises were the mark of his father's embarrassment. After each beating, Marty would head out to woods to nurse his contusions and displace his revenge on the wildlife there. The first time he'd killed an animal and imagined it as his father was when he only twelve years old. His father had cuffed him across the face for "backtalk," splitting Marty's lower lip, the sting and swelling immediate as he ran sobbing from the house.

Broadacre Woods was over seventy yards from their home, ten acres of green belt land overseen by the National Trust. The site was a favorite with local ramblers and kids out on their Duke of Edinburgh Award schemes, but no matter what the reason people came to Broadacre, its tranquility soothed all souls.

For a time, it had certainly been anesthetic to Marty's domestic injuries from his father's rogue temper. In that summer of 1977, hiding in the foliage of Broadacre, quiet sobs sending shudders through his body, Marty spat blood from his battered lips and wished his father dead. The thought was bright and came with guilt, the latter emotion strong but not enough to be outshone by his primordial need to get even.

His breath came in short gasps, the quiet rage building. Then he'd heard the sound, a rustling in the undergrowth that stalled the breath in his throat and made his head swim, his heart suddenly ice-water in his chest. The rabbit had crawled from a bush moments later, its ears flat to its back, a hind leg trailing behind it. They were kindred spirits in that moment, two wounded souls seeking solace under the canopy of trees.

Unlike Marty, the injured rabbit was not quiet in its suffering; it gave out tiny squeals each time it moved. The animal's pain and fear became a focal point in the very second Marty's anger toward his abusive father was at its peak. He'd reached for the rabbit and broke its neck with a single twist of its head, but in his mind he wasn't putting an ailing creature out of its misery; he was snapping the neck of his own father, and the surge of power this act gave him was a dizzying sense of liberty he'd never experienced before.

Seconds later, with the rabbit limp in his hand, Marty had begun making plans to murder his father. And several years later, he'd almost succeeded.

The telephone on the cupboard next to the bed rang, startling him from his murky thoughts.

"Mister Woodhead," Jacob said into his ear. "It is time for aperitifs in The Seaton Suite."

The phone went dead before he could respond. Rubbing his brow, Marty made for the *en suite* to wash up. Within ten minutes, he was making his way downstairs, thoughts now turned to the excitement the rest of the evening promised.

The ballroom of Cofton Grange was situated on the ground floor, accessed by a wide corridor to the left of a sweeping stone staircase central to the main hall. The ballroom was a place of high white walls and deep cornices. Blanched and fluted stone columns supported the lofty ceiling. Huge chandeliers hung down like glimmering beehives, the crystal giving off multiple starbursts.

The dance floor took up more than half of the room; oak boards shimmered under the bright lights. Around this area, circular tables were laid out, tablecloths turning them into white puck shapes flanked by high-backed, gilded chairs with red velvet manchettes and seats.

A bar ran the length of one wall, before which stools were placed at sociable intervals, and several feet away, a row of low cartouche tables ran parallel to the drinking area. At that moment, two people were perched on stools sipping vodka tonics. The bartender had served them and gone off to find more ice, and his only patrons chatted amicably, their excited voices bouncing around the walls.

Pippa and Antonia Okill sat near each other on the stools. Antonia's legs were long, her brown combat pants pinned to her trim waist with a thick leather belt, the silver buckle fashioned into the head of a snarling panther. The chiffon blouse was lime green with a halter neck, and her thick, black hair fell into stark curls about her bare, pale shoulders.

"And I told him that you spell it O-K-I-L-L, and there ain't no goddamned apostrophe," Antonia was saying. "Man, that guy was as thick as frigging custard."

In contrast, Pippa was slightly smaller; her hair wasn't wanton. Instead, it was pulled up into a bunch and pinned with long grips that looked like tiny daggers. She wore black cargo pants and a white t-shirt. "Why can't people get our damn name right?" Pippa said with a frown. "Is it that hard?"

Antonia winked. "Well, that was the next question I asked him. I've got to say, there's a guy to go to if you ain't there for intellectual conversation."

Pippa laughed in disbelief. "You are such a whore, Antonia Okill!"

They both clung to each other as they giggled.

The Okill sisters were not sisters at all. They were, in fact, first cousins but had been raised together when Pippa's parents had been killed in a freak accident while on vacation on the coast, something to do with a high wave and a low wall, the news reports had said later. Pippa was three at the time, and her Aunt Clair and Uncle Armand, her father's brother, stepped in to raise her. At six years old, Antonia had bonded with her younger cousin, giving her support and relishing having someone else to play with in the family home. They'd become inseparable—insufferable Clair and Armand often joked—during the course of childhood, though the relationship was to become far deeper as they grew into young women, especially after a coronary snuffed Uncle Armand from the earth, leaving Aunt Clair to draw comfort from her daughters to the point of suffocation.

It was during this time the family ethic became stronger than drive and ambition. "Without family, a person has no purpose," Aunt Clair would say over her second bottle of Chablis. By the time she died of liver sclerosis three years after Armand had departed this mortal coil,

Aunt Clair was on two bottles of scotch a day. She left behind not only two young, grieving women, but also debts large enough for Pippa and Antonia to be left penniless. Solace came from an unlikely place, an estranged relative they knew only as Uncle Roger, Armand's brother, who no one in the family would ever discuss, let alone invite to family gatherings. When an opportunity came to bend a few rules to make sure they would be secure forever, Uncle Roger was there offering a solution, and the sisters jumped at it.

Family was family after all.

A polite cough made them turn their heads. The barman had returned and was waiting patiently for acknowledgment.

Antonia sat upright. "Okay, you got our attention, fella. What we gotta do now, read your mind?"

If the bartender was embarrassed, there was no sign of it. "Mister Rothschild and the other guests are waiting for you in The Seaton Suite, Miss. Can I show you the way?"

He turned and headed off without waiting for a response.

Pippa slid off of her stool, eager to follow. "If that guy didn't have a broom up his ass, I think he'd be living in a bucket."

Chuckling, the women followed their stoic guide.

Oscar Jarman took a sip of his *Macallan In Lalique*, 65-year-old scotch whiskey, savoring the smooth heat in his throat and the weight of the lead crystal tumbler in his hand. The Macallan came in at just under fifty grand a bottle, the Waterford crystal tumbler around nine hundred pounds per glass. He loved the finer things in life and had always known they would come to him.

In his guestroom, he was surrounded by the kind of affluence he always felt he deserved. Refinery and grandeur came in abundance, the furnishings lavish, and the setting oozing with history. He felt content here; he felt *at home*.

Oscar had always felt bound for greatness. His origins did not give a hint to this, a small boy born to a civil servant, his father a mysterious figure in the British consulate in Hong Kong. His mother's affair had been brief, but the responsibilities she came away with were to be lifelong. No sooner had she'd made known her pregnancy, her consulate lover became very busy, meetings taking up his time from that day forward.

She got the hint after several weeks of trying to get hold of him. She'd returned from Hong Kong, back to the small mining village in The Rhonda Valley, mid-Wales, where she stayed with her parents until Oscar was born, a bastard yet still loved, supported by his mother and grandparents.

When Oscar was six years old, he stumbled upon his mother and grandparents having a heated discussion in the parlor of the small miner's cottage he'd called home for as long as he could recall. The argument had stopped as soon as his presence was known, his grandfather coming over to him to scoop him up in a playful hug and taking him outside into the garden, where a low hedge separated them from the rolling hills of the Rhonda Valley beyond. But Oscar's sensitive ears could hear his mother and grandmother starting up again as soon as they thought he was out of earshot.

The next day his mother began to search for secretarial work but could find nothing locally. She went further afield, determined to raise her son independent of her parents. It was only as he got old enough to understand such things as guilt and shame that Oscar realized his mother was fundamentally embarrassed by her upbringing. When she found work across the English border, working as a PA for a local mental health trust, Oscar's mother began to rebuild their lives, but the foundations were laid on grandiosity and self-delusion.

What they'd lost became the mantra for what they deserved, and yearning fueled delusions of grandeur. Before long, Oscar's mother was insisting that their humble beginnings did not define them; had fate not been so cruel, they would have been schmoozing with ambassadors and ladies, lower-echelon Royalty, perhaps. Oscar absorbed her woes, and over time, it sculpted his ego, shaping his outlook on life until he believed the aspirations to be real. By the time he was in his teens, he was telling anyone prepared to listen that his absent father was an ambassador who had died in a car accident. He came up with stories that he told with conviction because, in part, he wished it so hard it became real to his very own psyche.

He became articulate and smooth, creating a persona as convincing as the lies he told. He was to become extraordinarily rich over time, but the achievement—like so many things in his life—belonged to someone else.

That someone went by the name of *Georgina Cox*.

With the thought of the woman who had made all of this possible still rattling around his head, Oscar showered and clipped his beard. Then he headed downstairs, where more of the trappings of wealth awaited him.

Just as Jacob had requested, the guests were assembled in The Seaton Suite, an elegant drawing room three doors away from the grand ballroom.

The suite was resplendent, all of the furnishings a sanguine mix of pastel blues, yellows, and white. A huge fireplace was embedded in one wall, the white marble surround was ornate and speckled with veins of gray. Above it was a huge landscape painting depicting a fox hunt, the images of riders almost caricature; the horses were disproportionate with their large bellies and small heads, the huntsmen majestic in bold colors of reds and white.

Opposite the fireplace was a large window, wooden frames painted white and opening out onto the clinical, ornate gardens. The uprights embedded in the gravel paths turned this baroque place of ferns and bushes into an eerie netherworld of jagged shadows and stark white light, the ambiance helped in part by the bloated moon hanging in the sky.

Between the fireplace and the window was a social space that spoke only of opulence. Twin Chesterfield sofas of rich, red leather sat at ninety degrees to a half-height rosewood table. On this table were three silver buckets, each with its own bottle of *1998 Dom Perignon Brut.* A squad of flutes stood at attention, a selection of delicate canapés keeping them company.

Marty and Oscar were standing, each eating canapés served by Sanders. The Okill sisters had parked themselves on a Chesterfield sofa and looked very comfortable indeed. Pippa enjoyed sipping champagne while Antonia quaffed a *Coors Light* directly from the bottle.

Since coming into the room, the group had exchanged pleasantries in muted conversation, but there was an atmosphere about them, their conversation guarded. To an outsider, it may have come across as the awkward exchange of strangers. Instead, it was the stilted banter of competitors before a great race. They all knew of each other, their names synonymous with the best in their profession. And they were the top of their field because of the very reason they had been called together.

They had no limits.

The room fell silent as the door opened and Jacob stepped in. He crossed the room, his face measured, a small smile playing on his lips. He appeared as a man who is comfortable with his surroundings.

A man who was in complete control.

Walking to the back of the nearest sofa, he placed both hands upon the smooth leather. "Good evening, ladies and gentlemen," he said in a smooth voice. "And welcome back to Cofton Grange."

Chapter Two

Sanders was not a waiter. Sure, he carried himself like a member of the serving staff because maybe he often sat in cafes as a child watching his divorcee mother wait tables for a minimum wage. Perhaps it was due to the training he'd undertaken before coming along to this latest job. Either way, Sanders—aka, Detective Constable Ian West—left nothing to chance. Sloppiness got you caught, and for an undercover cop, the judge and jury came with a Glock 17 and wood chipper.

Ian had been with the police for over eighteen years. For a decade, he'd worked eight jobs and had eight personas that had been cultivated to perfection. At that moment, he was Sanders the Waiter, a position he'd held for ten months, and he'd served drinks and canapés to all manner of visitors just so he could get enough evidence to nail Rothschild's ass.

The Grange had often walked the line between blue sky and dark underbelly. Its prestige was outward-facing, the opulence, the history, all mesmerizing to the high-class consumer. Most of the groundwork had been laid down by Rothschild, a man who was known to be a master of misdirection, keeping his business affairs clandestine and off the radar with the help of a convoluted international network of shell companies.

These business dealings were painstakingly quiet, but they still made the kind of murmurs that got them noticed. Alana O'Shea was one such murmur. The informant, a chambermaid working at The Grange for over five years, had been passing on intel about activities at the house for the past three months before the police were confident enough to get authorization to infiltrate and investigate. It was her information that helped Ian and his support team to build his guise, crafting the kind of employee that served everyone's purpose, literally. His background was robust: a broken home, wayward youth who sought to eventually better himself after doing time, settling for waiting tables at numerous restaurant outlets, all with solid references. There was a plant in his file, a note from his faux parole officer suggesting that, while making good progress, the man who would be Christopher Sanders was prone to the influence of others from the criminal fraternity. It was buried deep, but not so deep that a security check by someone who knew what they were doing wouldn't find it. And the recruitment team at The Grange had indeed found it, as all back at police HQ hoped they would.

Once on the inside, there would be rules. Nothing was to be spoken, no covert conversations on the premises. There was only *Pink*, a code name for a dry stone wall where a large rock hid a cavity where intel could be passed on via simple cipher codes. It was an amusing play on Pink Floyd's "The Wall." The cryptic nature of the ciphers wasn't anything clever. Just enough to buy the person who put it there some time if it fell into the wrong hands. The kind of hands that would ball into fists or close around a throat until answers or death came forth. Death would certainly be an outcome regardless of how things turned out.

Yes, there were rules, but this time Ian had done something pretty damn stupid.

He hadn't meant to fall in love with Alana; hell, he'd done his damnedest to avoid any chance of that happening. This kind of situation led to bad judgment, poor decisions, and, above all, a loss of focus. The endgame was Rothschild, and he couldn't be diverted from that, but Alana *had* distracted him, and in some part of his mind, he took comfort from it, rationalizing that it was more natural if members of staff fraternized.

He almost gagged on his own bullshit.

In all of the times he'd been undercover, this had been the first where such a thing had happened. It was unprofessional; he knew this, but it didn't stop how he felt. As Ian walked, he recalled the first time they had kissed. It had been after a particularly long night of service; a group of dignitaries from some distant shore had partied hard and finally collapsed, sated in the late hours of the morning.

Ian and Alana had been clearing away the dishes when

they had both reached for the same dirty wine glass. Their fingers had touched, and he'd found himself looked up at her, their smiles mutual. Then the moment was upon them; it felt instinctive, it felt *right.* They made love later that same morning, the first and only time it had happened since he had been in The Grange; her caress had been exquisite, like no other he'd ever felt.

Traditionally, his relationships ended badly. He used to say the job didn't allow for such things, that he played so many roles it was hard for anyone to find the real person at the end of the day. But his love life had been pretty much shit *before* he became a police officer; his heart was never really into the demands that having a relationship required. Tracy, his ex-wife, would certainly testify to that, he was sure. Thank God there had been no kids to be dragged through his life of indifference.

Alana was different because she made *him* feel different. She made him want to care; she made him want to change. So as painful as it was, they agreed to restrain their relationship, put it on hold until after charges and convictions were brought against their paymaster. They knew it was the right decision; nothing could compromise either their safety inside these walls or the potential to put away the bastard who was Rothschild once they got their evidence against him.

Tough but necessary, and it was the only way forward. What had come out of it, apart from finding someone he connected with, was that Ian knew this job was no longer for him. It was time to get out of this covert world. More often than not it left a stain on him, one that sullied his psyche, so every day this gig went on, he knew it was bringing him closer to the end of his furtive career. He'd settle for a desk job thereafter, Alana with him. Perhaps they'd even raise a family. They had talked about it briefly and were in tune with the idea.

He made a conscious effort to focus on the here and now. The new life was some way off, no matter how much he craved it. And there was a nest of vipers at The Grange that could snatch it all away in an instant.

As he stepped out of the drawing room, Ian's amicable demeanor slipped away. He'd not seen or heard from Alana so far that day, but he wasn't concerned. This had the hallmarks of her lying low for a while, and this would mean Pink was harboring intel. He made his way down a wide corridor, the plush burgundy carpets soft beneath his loafers, the stark white walls interspersed with paintings that depicted huntsmen roaming the oiled landscapes, on foot and on horseback.

With a grim countenance, he looked about him to make sure all was clear before making his way to the lower conservatory, a south-facing hall with walls of plate glass and a huge seating area full of wicker furniture and tall ferns corralled in terracotta pots. The fronds reached up to the ceiling, their spidery shapes looking like dark specters blaspheming at the heavens. He could not help but feel this was an omen, and he shivered. The moment passed, and he cursed his apprehension.

"Get a damn grip, man," he whispered.

He coasted through the gloom and found the side door. Once outside, he slipped into the night, but try as he might, he could not prevent an ominous feeling from coming back to keep him company.

He moved through the moonlit landscape, the grounds breathtaking under the lunar glare.

There is beauty in this world, he thought. An image of Alana came to mind as though kicking against his need to keep on track. He sent it packing, looking ahead to the top of the wall that ran like a silver streak across the landscape.

While the guests enjoyed cocktails, Alana was folding the bed linen for each guestroom into neat rectangles, the edges as sharp and straight as a machine-tooled piece of plate metal. She placed these sheets into a large ottoman at the base of the four poster bed, taking pride in every action, a trait she had inherited from her hard-working parents.

She was the daughter of Edward and Margaret O'Keefe, who had lived in England for over forty years, having migrated from Cork, Ireland when her father had come in search of work in the steel yards of Sheffield back in the 1970s. They'd brought their six children over with them, Alana being the oldest of two sisters and three brothers, and her dedication to family life was total. She never strayed from home and embraced the warmth and joy her family provided.

Until she met her future husband, Dermot O'Shea.

He was a dandy, a man with handsome features and quick wits, easily winning over the heart of an innocent and impressionable young woman. They courted for only a few months and were married within the year, much to the chagrin of her parents. Dermot came with a reputation for gambling and connections with local gangs, but Alana was not to see any of this until she was so much in love that it was far too late to do anything about it.

Her husband's true nature came when they had their daughter, Crystal, and he spent more time at the tracks than at her side. Despite how much her parents insisted she should allow them to help her, she rebelled and ostracized them, choosing instead to live in the bubble that was to become O'Shea family life until the night her husband came home, face beaten, and one arm fractured.

He told Alana that they would be moving south to a place called Cofton Grange, where he had made promises to work as a chauffeur for one Jacob Rothschild. When Alana refused to move, Dermot became angry, and in his frustration, she saw fear. Questioning him, Dermot made it clear that he owed his new employer significant amounts of money and had agreed to work off the debt rather than pay for it in far more sinister ways. But Rothschild wanted to keep his investments close so they did not stray. Alana knew this now.

And Dermot *had* strayed. Even with all of the shit he'd brought to them, he'd tried to use a rival bookmaker to accrue more debts, not only defaulting on his deal with Rothschild, but placing his employer in a compromising situation when the bookie came looking for his money. By that time, Alana and her daughter were part of Cofton Grange; she considered it their home. Crystal was six when Dermot sealed all of their fates.

Rothschild had made good on his promise; he brought retribution of the cruelest kind, a punishment that served as a warning to anyone who would cross him. And in that week Alana experienced physical and emotional pain the likes of which she'd never known.

She still bore the scars; her psyche was strong, but on occasion, when she thought too much about those days when Rothschild got even with her family, she felt her resolve slip a little.

And the sense of isolation would come rolling in like an icy wave.

But her resolute nature had been honed by the resilience of her parents. Rather than give up, she made the decision to fight back, to get even with those who had caused her so much anguish. She'd been in a dark place for quite some time, and now she had found light, the light of hope and the means to bring down the cause of so much suffering.

Rothschild.

It had taken all of her courage to reach out to the police and offer her services as an informant. For the first month, she'd expected to find one of Rothschild's men at the door of her quarters ready to take her for a reckoning. But that had not happened.

What did happen was Ian West, a savior who had quickly become in tune with her. Yes, she accepted that she was a means to an end; to begin with, he was undercover and she was the source of potent information on the workings of The Grange. But it soon became apparent that their connection was far deeper than that of a working relationship. She doubted that either of them had expected such a thing to happen. But happen it did, and it was the only thing that kept her going.

There was a quiet knock on the room door.

"Come in," she called.

The door remained closed. The knock came again, and she went to the door with a bemused smile on her lips.

"Is that you, Ian?"

The man standing in the doorway wasn't Ian West, but Alana knew that her lover was the reason why she now had a hand clamped over her mouth to stifle her scream. She was shoved into the room; the door slammed shut seconds later.

Reckoning, it seemed, had finally come calling.

Rothschild scanned the drawing room and observed his guests. Both women were fidgeting in their seats, the glasses in their hands now empty. Oscar had taken to shifting his weight from one foot to the other, the crease in his forehead deepening as a frown settled in on his face as Marty began clucking his tongue like a cooling engine.

They're getting restless, Rothschild thought. *This is a good thing. This is what will make them stay the distance.*

He went to the fireplace, and his fingers traced the alcove in the surround. There was a small click, and the canvas dropped back into the heavily gilded frame before rolling upward to reveal a TV, its screen fizzing with static.

Marty smirked. "Nice trick. You got Thunderbird One under the swimming pool, too?"

Rothschild gave a cordial smile. "I'm afraid not," he said. "We have something far more impressive."

Placing his drink on the occasional table, Oscar walked up to the screen. His eyes squinted as though trying to see beyond the oscillating pixels. "Hopefully it'll be worth the money I paid to get a look-see."

Rothschild's demeanor remained genial. "Such things are always relative, Mister Jarman," he said in a smooth tone.

Oscar shook his head. "Well, at a hundred grand, this was *relatively* expensive, and it had better be worth it."

"Anyone would think that kind of money is out of your league, Oscar," Antonia giggled. "If you can't keep up with the stakes, maybe you should've stayed in that shitty little town you grew up in."

"Watch your fucking mouth," Oscar snapped as he took a step toward the sofa.

Marty blocked his path, his hands in the air as though warding off evil. "Easy there, chief," he said. "You're not going to let these witches rile you up before we know what's on offer here, are you?"

There was a fire in Oscar's eyes, but it was tempered

by Marty's words. He took a huge breath and let it go before moving to the opposite side of the room.

"Let's just get on with it," he growled.

"Very well," Rothschild said. "But first, let me begin by telling you some things you may already know."

Oscar sighed. "Do you *have* to?"

Jacob pressed on. "You are all here because challenge and competition are elements that define you." His words were clipped and delivered as a statement of fact. It was effective; his audience all nodded as if on cue. "So it is that you are all attracted to the taboos associated with your craft. You hunt that which society says you should not. The rare, the dangerous, the sacred."

Oscar raised his glass. "That's a fucking fact, make no mistake. Good things come to those who *bait*, right?"

Antonia wrinkled her nose as though she'd found something bad in the air. "Good thing you can shoot straight, Oscar, 'cause you ain't making no living out of comedy."

Oscar shrugged his shoulders. "Who cares? This line of work pays better."

The group nods were back, and Jacob was speaking again, his hand now reaching inside the pocket of his suit. He removed a slim, rectangular remote control, the sliver of silver stark against his weathered palms.

He pointed the remote at the TV, and the static immediately disappeared, giving way to a clear image of a man. He was naked, his right ankle shackled with a heavy length of chain to the walls of a bleak stone cell. Bars of a cage framed the scene, and the frantic pants and moans of the figure scrabbling around the cell floor provided the soundtrack to his suffering.

"You got this on RTL?" Marty chuckled.

Oscar was less amused. "What the hell is this, Rothschild? I'm not here for some kind of freak show."

Jacob held up a placating hand. "Oddities and curiosities are indeed for cheap fairground attractions. What you see on this screen is far beyond such things. This man is the *very reason* you are all here."

Pippa sat forward in her seat, her face nonplussed. "We've all done a *manhunt*. That kind of thing gets pretty old pretty quick."

"And it sure as hell isn't worth a two-million buy-in," Marty interjected. "Tell me you're adding some glitz to this party?"

Before Jacob had the opportunity to quell the growing mutiny of his guests, a loud, agonized scream cut through the room, making everyone but their host flinch.

All eyes went to the screen, where the naked man lay on his side, convulsing. His mouth and eyes were wide as he stared at the camera—at his audience—as though he knew they were all there watching his ordeal.

Every muscle, every sinew quivered under skin that was beginning to turn translucent. The man's dark, lank hair seemed to writhe of its own accord, a caged Medusa lashing out. The scream was gone, replaced now by a series of hoarse croaks of pain. But the major sound was that of multiple creaks and pops, a symphony of suffering that all too quickly became overlaid with terrible cracks and squelches.

Oscar moved closer. For a few seconds, his mouth mirrored the man on the screen. "What the hell is this?" he whispered.

No one replied. Instead, they all watched as the man on the screen changed. Limbs elongated, muscles bulged against skin until it started to tear. Instead of letting loose blood and tissue, wads of dark hair came forth like the legs of hideous spiders clawing to be free.

His face bubbled, the cheekbones seemingly becoming fluid, yet his upper and lower jaw moved forward, a pliable mass of undulating flesh until it formed an unmistakable muzzle. In his mouth, huge, sallow teeth punched through the gums, a wicked portcullis closing off the open maw. Blackened lips parted, and a great tongue of livid red slopped out onto the cell floor, a coating of thick saliva coming with it. Eyes of yellow flame seared into the screen, the rage in them as intense as their fixed stare.

The following seconds saw the body of a man disappear—skin now bristling with fur—the shackles clattering to the floor as the creature fiercely yanked at the chain and it gave way to the force brought against it. Like a newborn foal, the great beast rolled onto its paws and fought its way to its feet, the limbs jittering, fur slick with some unfathomable residue.

Then, if any of the stunned observers had any doubt as to what they had just witnessed, the great wolf let loose a huge and ferocious howl.

Ian made his way through the silver half-light. The walls of The Grange were splashed by the spotlights embedded in the driveway and reflected a diffused glow across the lawns, where it clashed with the great moon overhead.

He followed a run of acacias, their skeletal shapes providing both the perfect guide and enough shadow to keep his progress hidden from casual eyes. There was some CCTV coverage, but Pink was chosen because it had a blind spot that Alana had identified before he'd even set foot on the estate. Damn it, there he was thinking of the incredible, brave woman he'd totally fallen for and swore to save from the sinister world into which she'd found herself. At that point, all he knew of her past was from the pre-job intelligence his team had gathered. That she had an unspecified ax to grind with Rothschild, enough for her to offer to become an informant and risk her life in doing so. Ian had been cautious at first; the subtle intimacies she gave out made him wary, as though testing him. But ultimately, the woman was the reason he was able to infiltrate The Grange. It served no purpose to have him there if her intentions were not honorable.

As he moved through the trees, he thought about how he'd ended up doing what he did for a living.

Only it wasn't really a living, was it? It was a *life*, a "calling," if you will. There were no half measures when undercover; there was only belief in the character you played, internalizing every nuance until it became part of who you were, and Ian was exceptional at it.

For a while, he had considered acting as a career. In school, he had gravitated toward drama and found some escape from a bland home life in the productions. His parents were indifferent to most things; the greatest example of this was perhaps their marriage, which they seemed to move through like actors in the dullest play ever produced. They went through the motions, playing the role of parents until his mother's affair moved the genre from period drama to psychological horror. He figured that on some level he'd absorbed the ability to pretend from his parent's apathetic marriage. A sad reality, he had eventually concluded, but a reality all the same.

He fought for focus. It wasn't like him to dwell on a past that was part of his true persona. Then again, it wasn't like him to fall in love with a fucking informant either. Both were dangerous mind-sets, and he'd succumbed to them both with too much ease.

He became Sanders again and headed toward a small incline. Pink was at the bottom, shrouded in milky light. He scuttled sideways down the grassy slope, pulling a small Maglite torch from his pocket. He clicked it on, masking the intense beam with his fingers, creating a hazy vista ahead.

The dry stone wall snaked off like a crooked spine in both directions. He carefully navigated the incline until he stood by the uneven stones. They were haphazardly shaped and stacked six feet high, ending in large capstones that held the wall in place.

He looked in both directions before making for a

small bush several feet to his right. He crouched down, peered left, and counted the rocks from the ground upward until he located a small stone that rattled under his touch. He used the fingers of his right hand to wiggle the rock free, the torch now bright as he aimed it into the dark space beyond. Sure enough, there was a folded sheet of paper, which he retrieved. Then, placing the torch between his teeth, he unfolded the message.

At first he was confused, not because the message was written in a different code. It was because it wasn't written in code at all.

Ian's breath stalled in his throat as he saw the five words written in block capitals:

WE KNOW WHO YOU ARE!

Before the true implications could wash over him, Ian heard a click to his right. He knew it was a Taser before the three red dots made a triangle on his chest.

The last thing he sensed as the barbs were discharged was the metallic stink of cordite and the way his teeth chattered like the fear he could no longer express had found a way to have a voice.

Chapter Three

From the TV, a ferocious salvo of snarls and hideous barks cut through the drawing room. The stunned faces of those watching the creature pacing its cage were fixed with awe.

Jacob switched off the TV, and the silence was as shocking as the images they had all just witnessed. No sooner had he set the mechanism in motion to retract the TV voices began talking at once, all laced with excitement and incredulity.

But their host held up a hand and raised his own voice above the hubbub. "Ladies and gentlemen, if you please."

The chatter petered out, and Jacob cleared his throat. "It is at this point that you have exceeded the threshold of your deposit. The one-hundred-and-fifty-thousand was to view the prize, an agreement to which you are contractually obligated."

Pippa was now on her feet. "You saying we don't

get to ask what the hell we just saw?"

Marty rubbed his brow, still bemused. "I just saw a man turn into a fucking wolf. That's what I saw."

"We *all* saw it," Antonia said. "What I want to know is *how*?"

"I can neither confirm nor deny any further questions until there is *commitment.* And, as you know, that commitment comes at a fee of two million Great British Pounds."

Oscar's demeanor was bullish as he spoke. "How do we know that thing is real and not some kind of special effects trick?"

Jacob considered this for a moment. "Have I not always catered to your needs? You have hunted down snow leopards and white tigers on this land, have you not? Why would I short change such well-paying and loyal clients? It's not good for business. And I am a *very* good businessman."

Oscar fell silent, but it was fleeting. "Okay, Rothschild," he said, reaching into his pockets and pulling free a Smartphone. "I'm in."

The others began retrieving their phones, and Jacob grinned. "Once payments are confirmed, you can ask your questions. And I can lay down the rules."

"Rules?" Marty said with skepticism.

"There are *always* rules here, you know that. And given the special nature of tonight's prize, these are the requirements of the buy-in. But if you'd rather not?"

He allowed his inference to dance in the air for a while. It wasn't long—barely three heartbeats—before

Marty conceded.

"Then let's get down to business," Jacob said. "Then the real fun can begin."

Ian came round to the tinkling sound of running water. Diffused whiteness pressed against his eyelids even before he managed to ease them open. He found himself squinting at the starkness of the room around him.

As his eyes adjusted to the fluorescent lights overhead, Ian turned his head to see he was in a world of white walls and stainless steel tables. He tried to sit up but found his limbs secured to the table with manacles of leather and Velcro at the wrists and ankles.

At the far end of the room was a sink unit, and the faucet was splashing water onto the hands of the bald man in a white lab coat standing in front of it. To Ian, he looked like a stereotypical mad scientist, a simile his mind shelved as soon as he saw the incongruity of the jeans and training shoes below the hem of the lab coat.

The man turned, and Ian found himself staring into eyes of ice blue, magnified by thick lenses set in heavy black frames. The beard was dark, bushy, and peppered with gray.

"Hey, you're awake," the man said.

"What am I doing here?"

The man approached the table. "I think we both know the answer to that DC West."

"What the fuck you talking about?" Ian feigned indignation like an Olivier-award winner. "My name is Sanders. I'm serving staff."

The man dug into his coat pocket and pulled out a slip of paper. Ian recognized it as the note from Pink. "*We know who you are*," the man recited without referring to it. "Or have you forgotten?"

Ian continued the act. He had to, his role had no understudy. "I don't know what that means. And whoever's been talking shit about me is wrong, you hear?"

"That would be Alana," the man said. "She says you and her share a secret or two."

Ian fell silent; his eyes fixed in a cold stare. "You're lying."

The man chuckled as he pocketed the note. "We're all lying, DC West. But not Alana. Not *anymore*."

"What the hell have you people done?" Ian spat. His face was ruddy with anger as his wrists and ankles worked on his bonds.

The man studied Ian's futile attempts at freedom with a bemused expression. "Did you know your partner-in-crime has a six-year-old daughter?" he asked casually. "Her name is Crystal, and she has the cutest little button nose you ever saw, a real Pears Child. A parent would do anything for a child like that, almost as much as the serial pedophile we lined up to say 'hi' if Alana didn't sing like a bird. It took a while, though. But in the end, everybody came out of it with something. Don't you just love deals like that?"

"I love a deal where motherfuckers like you get to

sit inside a cell until they rot."

"Ooh, tough guy, eh?" The man considered Ian through his thick lenses. "I guess we'll find out soon enough."

"Are they safe? Alana and her daughter?"

"That depends on you."

"If you know I'm a cop, then you know that anything you do from this point on has consequences. You should let me up off this table, and right now."

"We both know that's not going to happen, right?"

Silence. It rolled out as all standoffs do, both men weighing their options, only one appearing as though he had all the time in the world.

"I need to know what you know," the man said. His pate glittered like jewels under the lights. "Or your informant and poor little Crystal will suffer, and it will all be on you. Nothing personal, as they say. It's just the way it is."

"You got a name?" Ian said. Time was short, but he was still trying to buy in.

"I got plenty. You'll be calling me all of them by the end of the night."

"How about you humor me for a bit?"

The man smiled. There was no warmth to it. "Okay, you can call me *Joe*."

"If you let me up, Joe, we might be able to do a deal. How does that sound?"

Joe laughed. "I already made the deal. Signed on the line, and there's no going back. You know how this goes. Reneging on an agreement means termination of the contract in a literal sense. And my body will be on permanent vacation at the bottom of a lake."

"It doesn't have to be like that," Ian said quickly as Joe momentarily lost interest in him and went to a small steel trolley at the foot of the table.

"It does, and it is." Joe scanned the contents of the trolley, his fingers tracing the glimmering stainless steel edge before he nodded and picked up an item.

A twinge of panic crawled through Ian's belly when he saw the surgical hammer. *Got to stay calm*, he thought. *In times like these, it's fear that gets you killed.*

"What do the police know of Rothschild's operation?" Joe asked. The smile was back. The hammer in his hand looked like it could inflict beautiful agony.

"Look, Joe, let's be transparent here. I want off this table, and I'm pretty sure you don't want to do anything that's going to put you in a cell for the next thirty years too afraid to take a shower."

"Answer the question, DC West."

"Joe—"

Joe rested the hammer on Ian's knee. "Well, seeing as we're being so *transparent*, I guess I'm going to have to tell you this next bit is going to hurt like a fucking bitch."

He lifted the hammer high and brought it down almost immediately. The crack of shattering bone was as loud as the agonized scream that followed it.

The online transfers took a few minutes, prepaid accounts sent money to multiple points around the globe, keeping them under the radar of international law enforcement. The group had migrated to a large dining room, where a huge table was set for a banquet. China plates and gold cutlery glittered under an eighteenth-century chandelier made of lead crystal.

Sitting at the head of the table, Jacob held aloft his wine glass and addressed his clientele.

"A toast, ladies and gentlemen," he said. "To the bold come the spoils."

Oscar grinned. "I'll drink to that."

The Okill sisters also reciprocated.

Marty remained reserved, peering down at his drink while deep in thought. "So are you going to give us some background on that thing in the cage?" he said finally.

Jacob smiled. "You are still reluctant to call it what it is," he said. "So I shall ease your discomfort. It is a *werewolf*, Mister Woodhead, a lycanthrope, a beast of folklore. Yet it is now as real as you and I. And you have paid for the privilege to try and hunt it down."

Marty looked up from his drink. "How is it possible?"

Antonia swallowed a sip of wine before piping up. "We all saw what happened. What does it matter how this glorious creature came to be in the hands of our host, or that it even exists at all?"

The silence that followed demonstrated an accord of sorts. Marty eventually gave it form by shrugging his shoulders. "Okay, you guys win. So, what are these rules we paid to hear?"

Jacob laughed. "All in good time, my friends."

He clapped his hands twice. The sound was loud and sudden enough to make them all start. A door at the far side of the dining room opened, and several serving staff filed in, their hands laden with trays.

By the time the staff got to the table, the guests were focused on the lavish spread that was laid out before them. They ate as though they had not seen food for an age, and the variety of fare on offer was as abundant as it was exotic. Wines came from France and Italy, and several bottles were quaffed during the hour at the table. These were seasoned drinkers as much as they were capable hunters. The sense of occasion added to all of their needs and desires.

Content and merry, the group sat back in their seats as the serving staff returned, a small army in black-and-white suits, clearing away the dishes with the efficiency of ants stripping away crumbs after a patio picnic.

Jacob tapped his wine glass, and the bright, little chimes brought the group to order. "Once we have allowed our meals to settle, then I suggest we retire to the cellar, where the next phase of the evening can begin."

"Shit, Rothschild," Pippa said, "I'm not going to be able to hit the side of a barn if I take any more grog on board. Think I'll pass."

Jacob laughed. "I seriously doubt that, Miss Okill. But you are quite right; we will not be going down to the cellar for more wine."

"Then what's in the cellar?" Antonia replied. An air

of tension entered the room. "Not that *thing*?"

"Definitely not," Jacob said. "Just the means by which you will be able to kill it."

Oscar sat up. "I usually have specific requirements for a hunt," he said.

Jacob stared him down. "I think we've established this is not your usual hunt, Mister Jarman. And I believe we said something about there being rules."

"Then how about you shed some light on those goddamned rules given we've paid in to hear them," Marty interjected.

They were all startled as Jacob suddenly stood. "Very well. Seeing as digestion is not a priority, I shall escort you to the cellar this very moment."

No one needed telling twice.

Chapter Four

At the age of ten, Ian had been riding his BMX over rough terrain at Arrow Valley Park in the Worcestershire town of Redditch. He'd been racing Edward Crane, his friend through high school who would later fall foul of an articulated wagon on the M5 motorway just off Junction Six for North Worcester.

Arrow Valley was a huge bowl scooped out of the earth, bordered by ash and silver birch trees, and in the basin was a huge lake, a place popular for walkers, joggers, and those out to fish for carp, bream, and perch. The boys had traversed the high grass and dirt embankments leading down to the lake when Ian had hit a rut and was catapulted over the handlebars, his hands still clamped on the handles as he landed heavily. Ed had rushed over to him, his face undecided on an expression as he approached. Finally, he settled on disgust as Ian sat upright and flexed both writs backward and forward.

"Man, you're bending those things like Mister Fantastic." Ed grimaced. "Doesn't that hurt *at all?*"

Ian had been equally surprised. "No, but I'm not going to moan about it."

He'd continued to flex his wrists, pushing them so far forward the palm of his hand was flat to his forearm. He did the same the other direction.

Then Ed had vomited on the grass.

At Ed's funeral, Ian was to tell this story, and it brought sad smiles to all at the church. But now, as Joe brought down the hammer, his intention to shatter Ian's left kneecap, instincts kicked in.

It had always been about keeping the guy talking; misdirection was a device when in a tight corner, after all. While Joe had been focused on his intimidating script he had become lost to the world about him, Ian had used both time and his double-jointed wrists to get his arms free of the Velcro cuffs.

Joe didn't know about this until Ian grabbed his arm on its descent. The hands clutched the wrist so firmly Joe cried out in pain and surprise and tried to pull away. But Joe's own momentum was against him, and Ian used it, dragging the man down toward him as he lifted his own head at a rate of knots.

He drove his forehead into the center of Joe's face. There was a shocking popping sound as Joe's nose gave way, his glasses shattering as they were rammed into his eyes. His scream was bright and thick with blood as it found its way down his gullet.

Ian pushed him away and then dragged him back again, where the forehead shattered Joe's left cheekbone and left stars before Ian's eyes.

The police officer shook his head clear and snaked his forearms about Joe's throat, yanking him so his back was resting against Ian's chest. Adrenaline coursed through Ian, making him tremble. They sat on the table, like lovers in an endless embrace.

"Where's Alana?" Ian hissed into his captive's ear.

"At the movies," Joe gurgled before the sleeper hold sent him to a place darker than his soul.

Puzzled, Ian shoved the slumped body off of the table, and it fell unceremoniously to the hard tiles.

He freed his ankles of their restraints and swung his legs off of the table. Dizziness came upon him, the effects of fifty-thousand volts from the Taser and, he strongly suspected, using his head as a battering ram. Across the room he could see his ghoulish reflection in the mirror; his face was pale and drawn, and a dark bruise was emerging on his forehead. There were also smears of Joe's blood on his cheeks and brow.

With caution he stood, waiting for the nausea and giddiness to pass. When it did so, he went to the sink unit and splashed shockingly cold water onto his face, clearing away the gore and reviving his senses. It was time to get sharp. He was under no illusion that he'd been lucky. Now he had to stay determined and stay alive. It was the only way he could help Alana and get the fuck out of here. He also needed to figure out what the hell was Joe talking about when he'd said "at the movies." There was nothing worse than a cryptic psychopath. At this thought, Ian looked at Joe's crumpled form. The man's face was a contorted mass of swollen tissue and free-flowing blood.

He went over to Joe and checked the guy's pockets. He found a mobile phone in the back pocket of the unconscious man's jeans. A strange clicking sound came from Joe's throat as Ian rolled him over to retrieve the device. The screen was cracked, but the phone had enough power to show the images of *Little Mix* on the lock screen.

Ian took the phone to Joe's right hand and placed his thumb on the print reader. The screen pinged alive, but Ian could see there was no service. He looked about the room and tried to recall if he'd ever received intel that a place like this existed on the estate. He parked the thought as another came to him. How long had the Taser put him out? Maybe he wasn't on the estate at all. Maybe he'd been moved off-site to somewhere that gave the kind of privacy an interrogation required.

His mind stowed these intrusions. This was ground zero, and he had to accept it. Communication was the key to it all. He had a phone, now he needed the means to get word out. But it would have to be a watching brief for the TAC team on the end of the line. If they came in before he found Alana, then she and her daughter would be dead in seconds. He thought fleetingly about Crystal and why Alana had not mentioned her. Maybe she was trying to protect her, trying to protect herself from rejection.

Now isn't the goddamned time to do this, he scolded his negative thoughts.

Ian went into the phone settings and switched off

the fingerprint reader and reset the passcode to his badge number, smiling at the irony. After he'd stored the phone in his pocket, he retrieved the hammer and made for the door, an obelisk of stark white with a round handle, which he turned. Tentatively, he pulled the door open and stepped through.

The corridor beyond was more of the same, clinical white walls and doors. He only hoped Alana was still alive behind one of them.

That thought got him moving.

True to his word, Jacob had led them from the dining room through to the main hall, where an angular door followed the line of the staircase above. A long run of steps took them deep beneath the house, where the basement became a series of rooms coming off a central square made of slabs of red brick. Some doors were marked in gilded stencil. One gave access to the wine cellar, another to the emergency generator room. Though no one repeated Antonia's concern, many still thought that behind one of the doors an incredible creature was caged and waiting for release.

Jacob had taken them to a plain-looking door made from solid steel, and to those standing on the threshold, it was as though they were about to step inside a bullion vault. Inside, there were no shelves stockpiled with gold ingots. However, there was a bench with six items resting upon it.

Oscar looked at the items on the long bench in disgust. "What the fuck are those?"

The halogens overhead made even the blackest metals gleam like sunlight on an oil spill.

"Crossbows," Jacob said as he patted the weapon nearest to him. He placed a hand on a sheath of brown leather. Several black feathers stuck out from the top of it as though a crow had sought solace from the bright overhead lights. "And a quiver of bolts," he added.

Oscar's tone was brisk. "What kind of BS is this?"

"The kind that gives kudos to the one who kills the beast?" Antonia suggested.

Jacob smiled. "Miss Antonia is correct, of course. If this were your average hunt, then perhaps high-powered rifles would be the order of the day. But as we've established, nothing about this hunt can be considered standard. It is, by definition of its existence, a unique event. And as I have said before, there has to be rules. You bought into that idea, remember?"

Oscar pulled a stern face. "I went into this blind, and you know it."

"You are under no obligation to stay," Jacob said. "The money will be returned to you minus the one-hundred-and-fifty-thousand. That applies to you all. You have all signed non-disclosure agreements. Not that anyone would believe in the existence of such a creature. Your credibility would certainly suffer if you felt it appropriate to share the events of this evening to the world."

"You think we'd ever do such a thing?" Pippa

sounded indignant.

Jacob's face remained indeterminate, but his voice was low and sinister. "Before the apprehension on show tonight, no, I would never have considered it. Yet, now I think there may be a breakdown in communication. It concerns me. And in our business, concerns require *administration*, contingencies put into play to protect our exclusivity."

The threat was clear, and every one of them knew the man running the show had the means at his disposal to make good on it.

Antonia stepped forward. "Let's not go jumping to conclusions here," she said. "I can't speak for the guys, but me and my sister are definitely in. Rules or no rules."

Marty concurred with a vigorous nod.

Jacob turned to Oscar, and the others followed suit.

Disgruntled but yielding, Oscar stared directly at their host. "Yeah. Okay, I'll stay at the table."

Jacob's demeanor changed as though he'd just heard great news. He clapped his hands together like an excited child and patted the leather quiver again.

"Then we are back on track," he said. "We have three hours before we can begin the hunt. And the means by which you are able to snag this incredible creature rests here."

"What's that, a quiver of silver bolts?" Marty mused.

"The beast can be killed by conventional means," Jacob explained. "Though there are five bolts with silver shafts just so you feel confident in your own well-being if you are the one who tracks it to its end."

"You got any research materials on this animal?" Marty asked. "Not sure about anyone else here, but I like to know what I'm hunting and how it behaves when it's cornered."

"In the quiver is a burner phone containing all the information you need, as well as the expected rules of engagement," Jacob confirmed. "From this point on, there are no personal devices allowed in the hunting zone. All personal effects are to remain in your rooms. Are we in agreement?"

They all agreed, caught in the excitement of the moment.

Jacob looked at his watch. "In three hours we will let the beast loose on the estate. You have until then to get to know your quarry."

Pippa let out a sigh of contentment. "I still can't believe what it is we're hunting. It's simply fantastic."

Jacob's countenance became serious. "If you remember nothing else from the research I have provided for you, then know this—this beast is not only fantastic, it is extremely dangerous."

Pippa's eyes were dark and her smile cold. "So are we."

Outside of the infirmary, Ian found that the intermittent doors on either wall went on for as far as he could see.

"What the hell is this place?" he whispered, looking

both ways before making a decision to head right. His footfalls gave out thick sounds as he moved, the squeak of his soles on the tiled floor adding to his frustrations. He carefully tried the steel handle at the first door he came to but found it locked. This was the same for each room he tried to access for the next thirty yards.

He held the hammer in his hands, elbow bent as he approached each door, just in case someone suddenly emerged, or one of them was unlocked and he found himself confronted by another of Rothschild's psychopathic henchmen.

As he made his way down the passageway, Ian tried to recall any signs that indicated The Grange had a place such as this in the grounds. He knew the house very well, but Rothschild's clandestine activities required a degree of discretion, and this would require a level of environmental support that he'd clearly missed.

Why didn't Alana tell me about this place? The thought dropped into his head like a bad penny in a savings account.

His second thought came to her defense. *Maybe she didn't know about it. Maybe only Rothschild's trusted inner circle were aware.*

Yeah, but what if she sold you out? She never told you about any daughter, a dependent that was likely to be at risk if she collaborated. That's not the usual behavior of an informant, is it?

No, it wasn't. Not in his experience thus far. He was torn between his feeling of concern for Alana's safety and the greater terror that his feelings for her had been misguided, that it had all been a ruse, a means of catching him off of his guard to blow his cover to those watching.

These doubts stalled his steps, pulling him up short of a door on his left that suddenly opened inward with a swish of air. The man who came through was tall and wide, the shadow he cast on the floor oozing before him like an oil slick on the crystal waters of paradise.

Dressed in a navy blue coverall with a utility belt about his waist, the guard stepped into the corridor, his holstered baton and Taser bouncing against each broad hip. His heavy boots were black and matched his peaked cap. The Grange crest—a coat of arms with two lions facing inward and clutching a dotted shield—was sewn neatly into the cap in fine gold thread.

Ian absorbed all of this in the few seconds it took the guard to realize he was there. The hammer arced through the air, but while the guard was slow to register the act, he was fast enough to respond. He lifted an arm to block the assault, and the hammer hit him on the wrist with a satisfying crunch of bone.

The guard gave out an angry cry of pain but lashed out with his free hand. The blow caught Ian on the cheek, and pain flared hot and irate as though he'd been branded. He went spinning, the hammer skittering off down the corridor as he bounced off the wall.

The scene ahead looked as though he was watching the guard advance through a curtain of water, the baton raised, ready to dole out retribution. Ian shook his head, trying to clear his vision, and threw himself to the other wall as the baton whistled through the air near his head.

There was a loud report as the polycarbonate stave met the wall. Ian used the moment to launch himself at the guard, hands going for the fractured wrist, which he grabbed without mercy.

"Motherfucker!" the guard gasped as Ian yanked on the limb. The baton came at him, but he was ready, lifting up the guard's arm to counter it, and the strike was effectively blocked to the point of being useless.

In the melee that followed, Ian brought up a knee into the man's exposed groin; the contact was firm and unfettered. The guard's knees gave out as his good hand went to his balls, face twisted in pain. It was into this face that Ian brought his foot; the force of the kick snapped the big man's head back and sent him sprawling.

Ian went over to check the guard and nodded in satisfaction when he concluded he was out cold. He checked the utility belt and removed it, leaving the guard on his side. He strapped on the belt, comforted by the weight of the packs and Taser. After securing the buckle, he retrieved the baton from the floor and headed to the room vacated by the guard.

He went inside, confident that it would be empty given that no one had come to the guard's aid. Sure enough, the room was unoccupied; the only signs of life came from the images on the banks of TV monitors built into the far wall of an otherwise bland room.

Ian dragged the guard into the room and dumped him to one side before closing the door.

He walked toward the monitors, each served by a small console embedded into a lectern of chrome and glass. Several lights and dials flickered as the CCTV screens ran through a predetermined cycle.

He gazed at the rectangular images, the contents of which almost allowed him to forget his aching cheek. The CCTV showed a multitude of animals, all caged. He saw lions, tigers, and bears (oh, my); he saw panthers and cheetahs and leopards. But it was one particular figure that caught his attention and had him blinking several times before he confirmed what he saw wasn't the result of a concussion.

In one of the cages was a huge wolf. And it paced its cage in agitated, soundless fury. But this was not the reason Ian stood mesmerized.

No, the reason he stared at the screen with total incredulity was because the wolf was pacing its cage on *two legs.*

Chapter Five

In the chamber beneath The Grange, Jacob sensed the rivalry in his guests and enjoyed the moment. He spoke in his usual even tone. "The rules are simple enough. In case you forget or choose to go 'off-piste,' the mandate is written into the information packet sent to your burner phones. Understood?"

All but Oscar mumbled an acknowledgment, who responded instead with an exaggerated sigh of impatience, which Jacob promptly ignored.

"The first rule is what you already *know*: the only weapon you can use is the crossbow. For balance, it comes with a pair of state-of-the-art night-vision goggles. There is also this." Jacob stooped and reached behind the bench. When he stood, he had a machete in his hands, the silver blade giving off a myriad of starbursts. "You may use this to finish off the beast and claim its head as your trophy."

"That's a fine-looking blade," Marty said in approval.

"Solid silver?"

Jacob nodded. "The second rule is you will each be allocated a zone on the estate. Each zone covers the same level of acreage, twenty acres to be precise. Into this area, the werewolf will be let loose for one hour at a time. It is a cyclical process; if no one bags the beast in their time slot, then it will go back to the beginning with the same order of play."

Marty appeared disgruntled. "So who goes first, and what happens if they make the kill before we get a chance to hunt?"

"Just as fate has struck down this creature, so it will decide who goes first," Jacob said. "You will draw lots. If the beast is caught, anyone who does not get the opportunity to hunt will receive a full refund, including their deposit."

The hunters relaxed a little, clearly satisfied with his response.

"The last rule is equally as simple," Jacob pressed. "No one is to disobey the rules. You are to stay in your zones. You will be notified by the burners when the beast is loose and it is your time slot."

"How the hell are you going to herd that thing into another zone?" Oscar said.

"That's for us to worry about," Jacob said. "But I guarantee it will be achieved. Now, unless there are any further questions, it's time to begin the hunt."

"About fucking time," Marty growled.

No one challenged his comment. Instead, they went to the table and collected their hunting gear. They filed out, delving into the quiver and pulling free their burner phones where the information packet told them all they needed to know about their quarry.

They disbanded to take in the data on offer, each silently reading and digesting the content. Although they had separated, they were unified in their amazement and disbelief. Such creatures should not exist; every fiber of their highly practical beings screamed it at each of them. But the CCTV in Seaton Suite was the beacon in a fog of doubt.

The "Man-wolf" had been a beast of lore for as long as there had been people on the earth, it seemed. Every culture appeared to have a variant on the myth. From the ancient Greeks to tribal Africa, from China to central Europe, the stories of people who could change into great beasts were in abundance. Whether this was by their own free will, like the shaman of Asian and Africa, or as a result of some vile curse, as with many European tales, was a point of contention.

Some suggested wearing a wolf belt was enough to evoke a change; others spoke of drinking water through which a wolf had walked. Then, of course, there was the curse of being bitten by another werewolf and the influence of the lunar cycle. It was all contained on their devices, and whether in their rooms or walking through the grounds, they each absorbed the content with both apprehension and excitement. The desire to be the first to claim the beast also grew alongside the curiosity. But this was what drove them all, what united them at that one moment in time—*the competition.* The absolute need to win was as ferocious as any beast they had ever cornered and killed.

Tonight would be no different. Or so they thought.

The CCTV monitors ran through their automated cycle, and Ian swore as the image of the creature changed to that of a snow tiger. Glancing down at the console, he tried to see if he could isolate the camera to retrieve the incredulous sight he'd just witnessed.

The console had three rows of clear plastic buttons, all numbered and illuminated with a yellow backlight. Each button was named with low-tech, red ticker tape. One row told him there were twenty pens somewhere on site, one of them holding the wolf.

The thought of the abuse an animal had to go through to perform in such a way was beyond Ian's understanding. He'd dealt with some lowlifes during his work, but this was a new level of trash. But he also knew an animal like that would fetch a pretty penny during a Dark Net auction.

The pens were also a giveaway to the activities scheduled to take place at The Grange that evening. It was an easy assumption to make why four high-profile game hunters were on the same site as pens full of endangered species. But part of him was frustrated that the penalties for such crimes were token compared to nailing Rothschild for murder and heading up a crime syndicate. He tempered these frustrations with the consolation that illicit activities such as animal trafficking would be enough to get him his warrant to search the premises.

As he surveyed the console, something caught his eye that was to take his mind off of police procedural wins. The bottom row of buttons indicated other parts of The Grange. He noted the cellar, the library, and the main reception areas, all denoted on ticker tape.

In the time he'd been at The Grange, the whereabouts of the CCTV monitoring station for the building had been a mystery. Now he knew why; it was housed in an area that was in itself clandestine. But at least he now knew this place was somewhere on the grounds.

One monitor in particular caught his attention. Its ticker tape moniker told him it belonged to cameras covering the cinema. It was a twenty-seat theater deep in the heart of the house, and Rothschild hosted private screenings for many guests, including industry professionals from all over the world. The premiers on show were, of course, stolen dailies from major studios, and the audience consisted of rival companies that needed the edge over their competitors.

Nothing could be proved, of course. Nobody was willing to testify, and in the grand scheme of Rothschild's services, just like his illicit hunting schemes, this kind of stuff was small fry.

Then something came to him: the gurgling words of Joe as he succumbed to the choke hold when Ian had queried the whereabouts of Alana.

"She's at the movies."

Ian hit the button and saw the image of the movie theater come up at the center of the bank of screens. All of the lights were on, highlighting two tiered blocks of dark leather seats in rows of two. A pair of security staff stood in the central aisle.

And sitting on one of the large leather chairs was the small, delicate figure of Alana O'Shea.

The woods were dense. Even with the bloated moon splashing light down upon the canopy, only small, silvery pools made it to the woodland floor.

A strong breeze tousled the trees, the leaves giving out an incessant hiss as boughs creaked like floorboards shifting in the summer heat. Through this landscape, Antonia and Pippa, recipients of the first hour of hunting, moved with caution, the sounds about them aiding their stealth. Both women had the night-vision goggles on top of their heads; the gear was a light but bulky necessity as they ventured deeper into the shadows.

Pippa walked alongside her sister, her face wearing a disgruntled frown. "How come you get the crossbow?"

"Because I'm the oldest, that's why," Antonia replied. "Besides, you get the blade and can claim the head."

"But you get to *shoot* it. And if what I read about werewolves is right, that head we take is going to be *human* by the time we get it in a bag. Can't exactly mount that fucker in the lounge, right?"

Antonia pulled up. "Look, let's iron this out now because we've got the chance of getting us a werewolf, right? Let that one sink in: an *honest-to-God werewolf*."

Pippa was about to speak, but Antonia pressed on. "Are we a team?"

"We're more than that; we're family."

"And do we always get the job done because of that?"

"Yes."

There was no hesitation in the response because the question was without dispute. They were always *getting the job done*, and it had all started when they made the decision to reclaim the inheritance whittled away by their grieving mother, Clair. Their Uncle Roger had seen to that, a spurious character who had enough contacts in the murk of the criminal world to get things done and be so far removed from the shit that nothing stuck.

As a family pariah, Roger was not to come out of the woodwork until Clair's funeral, where the true nature of debt was more than known. Their uncle had paid for the ceremony and vowed he would protect the girls from destitution, taking them in for a time while he made sure he put things right.

He never promised to love them, and he never promised to change their lives, but he did pledge to get them what they *deserved*. And he did this by using an arsonist, a corrupt fire investigator, and an equally bent insurance agent, a triad of shady characters that neither of the girls met. They did, however, feel their combined influence as the house was razed to the ground due to 'faulty wiring' and they received a payout of five-hundred thousand pounds. Their uncle took two-hundred grand and 'invested' it in what he called his 'international interests,' and within a year he'd deposited ten million into an offshore account. Then he told them that they were on their own unless they wished to continue with their investments, and during this time, the girls grew into wealthy women, seeking out pastimes to befit their ever-increasing lifestyles.

A safari to Africa featured as one of those experiences, and an illegal hunt for white rhino proved to be the birth of their passion for the sport. The illicit nature of the hunt gave them a thrill that outmatched the process, and it wasn't long before they began to invest wholesale in the illegal hunting industry. They never questioned it; morality was not on their agenda. They were survivors, and in this, they understood the nature of hunter and quarry and reveled in its mandate.

"So, are we good?" Antonia said.

Pippa reached over and rubbed her sister's upper arm. "Always."

Antonia smiled and then nodded toward the writhing trees. "Then let's go get us a werewolf," she said.

They found several tracks and bridle paths that gave passage through the trees, which they circumvented until the breeze was pushing at their faces, avoiding the possibility of their scent alerting the creature of their approach.

With only finite weaponry, they stayed together, their tactics at odds with their usual 'pincer' method, but this was the game, and they intended to play it hard.

Several hundred yards into the woodlands, Antonia stopped and hunkered down, Pippa following without question.

At their feet was a mound of shredded flesh and fur. Even through the speckled jade of their goggles, both women could see the white streaks and elongated snout of a badger. The head was a few feet away from the mutilated remains, and Pippa took a finger and dipped to into the mass. She brought her hand away rubbing her index finger and thumb together.

"Still warm," she whispered. "Fresh kill, no more than ten minutes old."

Antonia nodded and scanned the ground around them. It was easy enough to see that the leaves and soil were churned, indicating a creature of great size had claimed its kill. She also noted the trail of gore and disturbed earth leading off to the east. She pointed it out to Pippa with a finger.

"Guess we follow the breadcrumbs," Antonia said, standing up. Pippa wiped the blood on her khakis as she joined her sister.

"Think there's a gingerbread house at the end of them?" Pippa asked with a grin.

The growling came to them a few seconds later, a low, oscillating tone that froze their bodies instantly. The sound emanated from ahead, carried in on the wind. It was a dreadful sound, savage. But rather than showing fear, both women grinned at each other.

"That's fucking awesome," Pippa said as she started off down the path.

"And it's all *ours*," Antonia replied, starting out.

The growling was not sustained. Instead, it came at intervals and on occasions stopped for several minutes to the point where the women feared they had lost the beast despite the heavy tracks indicating the contrary. The deep, guttural roar would then return to guide them, and their goggles indicated a light source ahead, a flare of yellow splashed through the green scope, skeletal trees outlined by its intensity.

Antonia lifted her visor and took in the view. Sure enough, the tree line was sparse, and a faint light came from beyond it.

"There's a clearing ahead," she said as the growl came again, loud enough to stall them.

"Seems our Big Bad is not too far away either," Pippa said, her voice hushed.

Antonia raised the crossbow and clicked off the safety. "Let's go," she said.

With caution, they made for the clearing. The trees wavered as though alive, the breeze in their faces not letting up. When they reached the tree line, the women paused behind the trunk of a great oak.

"Well would you look at that," Pippa breathed.

There was a small building no more than forty yards distant, a solid, oblong structure made from timber, with a tin stove chimney rising like a thick, bent finger. The windows were dark, but there was a lamp hanging from the architrave of a small slatted porch.

"Guess there is a gingerbread house after all," Antonia whispered.

A sudden howl rang out. Long and forlorn, it drifted across the clearing, cutting through the noise of the rustling trees.

And at once the women realized a simple fact, but it was Pippa who voiced it.

"That came from *inside* the cabin."

"Damn straight," Antonia replied. "We got the fucking thing cornered without breaking a sweat."

Antonia went to move forward, but Pippa placed a hand on her arm, squeezing firmly enough to stop her.

"Hold up, Sis," she said. "Don't you think this is a little too easy?"

Antonia's face appeared baffled. "A win is a win, isn't it? We took out a white rhino in 1999 with an M82A1? Since when have you cared about how easy it is?"

Pippa chewed her lip. "This is different, and you should know that."

"What I know is we have a creature from folklore trapped in that cabin, and I'm taking it down. I thought you were good with this?"

"I am," Pippa sighed.

"Then get moving or get left behind, Okill. Time is wasting."

Antonia brushed her sister's arm aside and moved out of the tree line, keeping low as she headed for the cabin. Pippa followed, the machete held ready to swing if needed. It crossed her mind that even the broad silver blade might not stop the incredible creature lurking within the cabin, but, as always, the thrill such danger evoked had her heart pumping like a piston.

The women edged toward the cabin doorway. A snarl rose and fell like a snoring drunk, and Antonia had the crossbow aimed at the door, a black rectangle in the viewfinder.

Wary, they stood to either side of a short run of wooden steps that led up to the porch as the snorts and growls continued from inside. Now closer, they could see that the door had been smashed off of its hinges, the ferocity of the assault demonstrated by the pieces of splintered wood on the boards.

The darkness beyond the doorframe was absolute, not helped by the swinging porch lamp in the foreground that made the viewfinder struggle to adapt to the conditions. Climbing the steps, Antonia and Pippa took their positions, shoulders against each door frame.

Antonia swept into the cabin. She saw the wide, snarling mouth and glistening teeth immediately. The glittering eyes reflected the porch light, and instinct had her putting the bolt of her crossbow in between them.

Pippa's voice was suddenly in her ear. "Congratulations, you just shot a rug."

Antonia blinked, and the view through her goggles showed the bolt was jutting out of the snarling face of a bearskin that lay on the floor before a stove burner. She hissed in frustration and took another bolt from the quiver on her back, reloading with quiet efficiency. The main lounge area was a jumble of abandoned furniture made featureless by dust sheets. On the wall opposite to the wood burner was a bookcase. Three doors led off from the lounge, and before heading further into the room,

Antonia raised the crossbow as the growls continued from deep within the cabin.

"We can't be trapped in here with it," Pippa hissed. "Antonia, we need to wait for it to come to us."

"Check your watch," Antonia replied. "We're on a timeline. I make it ten minutes before our slot is up. It's now or never, Pip. You with me on this? I'm not going to be asking you again."

"I'm with you," Pippa said, though without enthusiasm. Antonia entered regardless, forcing the younger woman to follow.

Inside the lounge, Antonia scanned the doors leading off to the right. There were two of them, both ajar with no sign of a break-in. To the left was another door, but as with the main entrance, this too was torn asunder, and it was from the gaping maw left in the chewed-up doorframe that the growls came, ebbing and flowing like surf hitting the shoreline.

Antonia took a breath and eased up to the chewed-up door, her body tense and ready to react. Pippa watched her sister take aim and step into the gap. The gasp of surprise came mere seconds later.

"What?" Pippa said as Antonia stepped back from the doorway, her shoulders loose.

Antonia's face was a mask of contempt. "Take a fucking look."

Pippa stepped up and peered into the room that turned out to be a small kitchen with a stove and a rickety, wooden kitchen table that seated four. And on this table was a stereo system complete with two large standing speakers, through which the sounds of growling and breathing emanated.

"What the hell is this?" Pippa said. Her eyes never left the set up in the kitchen.

"I'll tell you what this is. It's not a hunt; it's a fucking circus, and we're driving the clown's car."

Realization dawned on Pippa, and her face became twisted with anger. "So this was a con all along! That bastard Rothschild was just after the money." She looked down at the machete clenched in her hand. "He's going to regret letting me have this blade."

"Let's just get the hell out of here," Antonia said.

Before she could take a step, the light from the porch disappeared, making them both cry out in surprise. At first, they thought the power had died, but then they saw the towering shape slowly unfolding in the doorway. The lamplight filtered through the hairy silhouette, edging the fur and making it appear like black fire.

Its snarl was as loud as a lion's, and yellow eyes glowed in the viewfinder.

Antonia lifted the crossbow. "This isn't a log cabin; it's a goddamned honey-trap."

The very next second, both hunters and hunted made their move.

Chapter Six

As he made his way through the woods, Marty tested the weight of the crossbow. Just like his competitors, he was familiar with using such a weapon. In some areas, there was no other way of hunting without alerting authorities and getting yourself shot by nature reserve guards.

There was something intimate about hunting with weapons like these, and Marty admired Rothschild's ability to know the nuances of his clientele. Hunting was primordial; it tapped into the very DNA of what man once was, and the crossbow was a testament to this construct. Man would do anything to protect himself and those he held dear. And he would do *anything* to survive.

Just like Marty had decided when he'd killed the rabbit and made the decision to end his father's reign of terror over the family.

In the months that followed his decision, Marty had thought of several methods to kill his father. He considered rigging his chainsaw to shed its chain, of weakening the rungs of the aluminum ladder that was used to clear out the gutters each autumn. There was also the notion of rewiring some of the plugs on the numerous power tools in the garage. All too obvious, and all likely to make sure Marty would be caught.

During this time, his father continued his drinking and serial abuse. One event included holding his son's head beneath the dank water of a trough when Marty swore after being stung by a wasp while on a family stroll through local farmlands. His mother had intervened shortly before Marty blacked out, earning her a shiner for the trouble. This event was to ensure Marty avoided learning to swim, but it also kept his focus on what needed to be done: to wipe his father from the Earth.

In the end, the best solution was the most obvious. Every third weekend, Marty and his dad would go hunting in Broadacre Woods. They would camp out on a Saturday night, and *dear dad* would get pissed on cheap Bulgarian lager, rant about how much he hated his life, his wife, and the shitty choices he'd made, which then took him back to his son and the whole "having fucking kids" gig. Marty, a captive audience, would have to sit through his old man's tirade and the brunt of the vitriol, and with each put down or caustic comment, his hate for his father would fester and grow.

Marty had been on enough of these trips to know how to shoot a shotgun. He bagged his first pigeon when he was ten years old. His father had told him it wasn't skill he possessed, but luck. Either way, he was competent with a gun and waited for a time when he was able to engineer the means to use it. And that time came soon enough.

There was a thunderstorm on the night that Marty put both barrels of a Beretta 687 into his father's face. It was after he'd beat Marty with his belt following two more cans of lager than usual. During this ordeal, Marty had found his face pressed into the earth until dirt clogged his mouth and nose, and for a few seconds, he thought his father intended to turn the tables and beat him to the finish line in committing murder. Then the thrashing had begun, the heavy leather belt biting into his back and buttocks, even through his clothing.

Between the beer and the exertion it had taken to dole out the beating, his father crashed by the campfire, his great belly flopping onto the ground like a hippo's cheek. Great snores seemed to be in competition with the rumbling thunder of the incoming storm.

Smarting from his injuries, his fury at its peak, Marty loaded the shotgun, tears hot against his cheeks. He'd hobbled over to his father's grunting form and aimed the barrels at the side of his head.

For one fleeting moment, Marty hesitated, and the first fat raindrops fell from the thunderheads high above. Perhaps it was the rain hitting his face, perhaps it was instinct, but his father was suddenly aware of him, and a hand came up to bat away the gun, just knocking Marty slightly off balance.

But it was far too late.

The blast was lost amongst a huge crash of thunder,

and the side of his father's head disappeared in a plume of red mist and flying bracken. Marty had staggered backward, rain and lightning painting the scene, and the realization that this monstrous act came with such an overwhelming sense of liberty that he felt giddy, a feeling he never wanted to end.

When he saw his father's huge chest heave, making it clear he was somehow still alive, he didn't feel horror or guilt or fear; he only saw an opportunity to prolong his sense of freedom. So it was that Marty made a decision to call it in as an accident.

He used his mobile, and even with the terrible weather, the air ambulance had scrambled and airlifted his father to the nearest hospital within forty minutes of receiving the call. Even as the trauma team attended to his father, they took in the beer cans strewn about the campsite and the reek of alcohol on their casualty's breath and included this in their status reports when they handed the patient over to the Emergency Room staff.

His father's suffering was to last for another five years. Massive brain trauma from the shotgun blast had left him in a vegetative state, only able to breathe through an intubation tube. Mental functions were nonexistent, and his remaining days were to be served out staring at the wall of his room at the care home. His mother met a good man who treated her right, and so Marty left her to it with blessings and love.

He continued to visit his father, of course, spending the time reveling in the man's torment. For hours he would sit there, gloating and whispering curses as he stared at what was left of his father's face—one eye and a mass of scar tissue, a head that looked like a Baby Bell with a bite taken from it. It was an outpouring of bile accumulated over years of abuse. And Marty relished every single second.

There was irony in that when his father actually died of pneumonia, Marty's tears of loss at the funeral were genuine. His chance to gloat and goad now at an end, all he had was memories of the night he made the decision and the night he put it into action. Both involved the taking of a life, a rabbit and a father, and there was parity in the hunt.

He continued the tradition, becoming a proficient huntsman and using each safari or illicit hunt to connect with key elements linked to the joys of ending his misery. And it was this feeling he carried with him through the woods now, energizing and sharpening his senses with each moment.

Marty was pretty stoked when Rothschild had come to inform him that it was his time slot; the relief that the Okill sisters had failed to bag the prize was amazing, and the odds had just ramped up in his favor.

He scanned the locale, his goggles a cumbersome but necessary evil. He'd had to adjust the head strap several times before they were secure enough to be practicable. The green fizz in his visor told him that there was nothing to see; trees were yielding nothing, just a shimmying vista that squirmed as though alive.

Continuing forward, the foliage became denser, forcing him to forge several paths, using the machete to help make headway. The thought he might get fined for damaging the environment came to mind, and he smiled. It wasn't like he couldn't afford the tab. He stopped, hoping to pick up a trail. A beast of that size couldn't hide its tracks for long.

To his left, he spotted another patch of bushes and, sure enough, he saw that something—something big—had forced its way through. He headed over to the bushes to inspect them further.

He paused in mid-stride. Through his visor, he could see the oscillating trees and shrubbery, but there was also something else, twin orbs of light two hundred yards out.

Eyes.

Watching me.

The thought was there in seconds, and he dropped to a knee, taking aim with the crossbow and thumbing off the safety in one fluid movement. He inwardly cursed the wind as it swirled about him, knowing he would have to make allowances for the shot. He was in the process of making this calculation when he saw the werewolf emerge from its hiding place, an inspired sight as it came pushing into the woods on its hind legs. The CCTV really hadn't done justice to its scale. Marty figured it was well over nine feet tall; its front paws were more like hands, each furnished with menacing claws.

Marty took all of this in as he willed his quarry to come closer. His wish was granted in part as the beast dropped to all fours with a heady snarl.

Then it charged.

Pounding the ground between them, churning up

leaves as it came, an implausible monster now made real powered toward him.

Marty should have been afraid, but he had no sooner scoped the beast when the cold feeling that usually came to him when he was about to make the kill-shot descended. In the scope, there was no werewolf, only a monster masquerading as a man, his father with balled fists or a belt or a water trough.

One hundred yards out now, closing in with every bound of those powerful limbs.

The crossbow was rigid, pulled in tight against Marty's shoulder. There would be no recoil, but this was to make sure he did not deviate from the calculations he'd made to deliver the bolt. With this trajectory, the silver shaft would strike the beast between the eyes, an instant kill. Marty's heart pumped with expectation.

Fifty yards now, the snarls and snorts a reminder of the savagery and wanton power that came with the thing bearing down on him.

At forty yards, Marty stalled his breath and pulled the trigger.

Nothing happened.

No bolt zipping from the crossbow, no momentary yelp of pain before the beast went crashing to the ground in an explosion of leaves.

Instead, the beast continued to charge, teeth and claws coming ever closer.

There was no time to work out what was wrong; there was only time to get the fuck out of there, and Marty did just that, turning and running, drawing the machete from its sheath at his belt, the blade heavy yet providing no assurance.

At his back, he could hear the deep, heated breathing, the snaps and snarls of the beast chasing him down. In his mind's eye, it wasn't a werewolf at all but the salivating savage ghost of his father ready for retribution before dragging his son with him to hell.

The trees were now his friend; he snaked around them, a natural slalom that allowed him to keep his distance and slow down the creature. But luck also featured in the process, and it ran out twenty yards later when he mistimed a turn; his left shoulder met the trunk of the oak tree he tried to navigate.

Inertia spun him, his head glancing off of a branch, but the contact still hard enough to make him see stars, the agony of a dislocated shoulder dimming for a moment. Then the fire was back in his joint and neck, making him cry out as he pitched headlong into the bracken.

And as he crashed through, the coarse branches raking his skin and face, the ground changed as the gradient dropped off, and Marty fell, limbs slapping and snapping as he rolled down a steep embankment until he landed broken and semi-consciousness.

Vision blurred, his goggles smashed and ripped cruelly away, his fogged mind could still see light in the distance, the shimmering moon reflected on the surface of a great lake. Even if he'd had the physical ability to continue his escape, the lake had made sure his fate lay in the paws of the beast.

He was vaguely aware of the distant crashes as something large navigated the embankment, then a dull *thud* as it landed on the ground nearby.

The shadow crawled across his shattered legs, his ruptured pelvis, his punctured abdomen, the beast rising like a dark sun on Doomsday, blotting out the moonlight.

Marty's watched the beast consider him, its yellow eyes alive with rage. There was something else there, too—a need to kill.

At that moment, Marty considered why he didn't feel any fear, realizing soon after that acceptance had an anesthetic all of its own.

Then the pensive air left the moment, and the great beast was suddenly upon him.

Oscar had entered the wood via the west, and a jeep had been provided to take him there. Once dropped off, his driver—a large man with a crew cut and thick-set shoulders—told him he would collect him once the hour was up.

"You'd best come with a trailer," Oscar had said. "Because I'll be bringing back the Mother of all passengers."

Now, in amongst the trees, he moved with caution, his mind tuned in to the task at hand, and that was to make sure he came out of this whole thing with the prize and subsequent prestige he was owed.

He was his mother's son for sure. In some ways, his

marriage to a woman ten years his senior was inevitable. Such was his mother's influence Oscar was ultimately defined by her. That many years later he saw her traits in his future wife, Mary Cox, only made his determination to marry her greater. Knowing from their first date that Mary's mother, Georgina, had amassed a one hundred million pound fortune from a hedge fund also flavored the prospect of a lengthy relationship.

Almost.

But it was enough. He'd learned to love Mary, and it gave him a life of wealth and access to tastes without limit. So convincing were his signs of affection, Mary had him sign a prenuptial agreement with a ten million pound waiver. The perfect safety net should anything go awry. But he could accept that and tolerate it for the sake of the long game.

And the long game was Georgina.

Once the marriage was established, Oscar dug in, and over the next ten years, he engineered the downfall of his mother-in-law. In that time, he put doubts in Mary's mind about her mother's mental health. These doubts were reinforced by hiding car keys, making plans to meet her and then not turning up and claiming no such arrangements had ever been made. This never would have had weight, but Mary, well-meaning and concerned about her mother's welfare, was also duped and went with it. She circumvented lawyers, made sure that Georgina's financial interests were handed over as she took on legal custody of her mother's assets on the grounds of diminished responsibility.

Then Georgina was living with them, where the deterioration of her mental faculties became more pronounced, the decline made faster as Oscar and Mary took over her life and starved her of independence. By the time a nurse was brought in to take over full-time care, the couple had legitimate access to over one hundred and twenty million pounds. Georgina was to die eighteen months later with only a nurse for company while Mary and Oscar celebrated their twentieth wedding anniversary by moving into a villa in Marbella worth ten million pounds. By that time, Georgina's daughter and son-in-law had siphoned off most of her fortune and buried it in property all over the world.

Oscar had the perfect life. A doting, wealthy wife who was at that moment in the penthouse suite of the London Savoy enjoying the peace and quiet as Oscar hunted fantastic beasts on a country estate.

A feeling of contentment almost blunted his hunting edge. He forced himself to get back with the program. There was no time for slacking off; this was the hunt of a lifetime, and as no one had so far caught the werewolf, he favored his chances.

He followed a path that led him deeper into the trees. He had his night-vision goggles, but these were up on his forehead. Rather than enhancing his vision, he found they hampered it, so he planned to use the moonlight filtering through the trees.

The crossbow was primed and ready; his mind was in a calm place, perfect for the hunt. He suppressed a satisfied sigh as he went on. Coming across the huge block of stone at the end of the path came as a complete surprise. So much so that he pulled the goggles down over his eyes to check what it was that he'd stumbled across.

It was a building, easily ten feet high and thirty wide, flanked by trees; twin stone angels stood to either side of a great stone door. On the archway over the door, the name "Rothschild" was etched in the stone with a coat of arms depicting lions and a starred shield.

Mausoleum, Oscar thought.

His steps slowed as he saw the door was ajar, revealing a strip of blackness not even the goggles could penetrate. Something crawled inside his mind, a memory of spending a long day locked in the pantry at his mother's house, punishment for some misdemeanor long since forgotten. The impact of that day still resonated with him on occasions when confined in small, dark spaces. A power cut in an elevator in the Wembley Hilton had him freaking out to such a degree, the staff had to call an ambulance at Mary's insistence. The paramedics came and gave him oxygen as a lobby full of people looked on.

Shuddering, he changed course and made to walk by the building, shrugging off the skin-crawling panic that threatened to surface. Taking several breaths to ease his nerves, he waited for his heart to calm.

On his last exhale, Oscar heard the deep, rattling growl from behind him, and it was close enough for him to feel spittle spatter his neck.

His true nature kicked in, and he moved, faster than most would have thought possible given his unhealthy lifestyle. He lumbered toward the mausoleum and the heavy door, the crashing and snapping of branches and foliage immediately behind him. The thump of paws on the ground spurred him on.

He thought about turning to get off a shot but dismissed this as a flight of fancy from a desperate mind. He concentrated on ramming his shoulder against the door; it swung inward with remarkable ease, sending him sprawling inside. The noise of his landing on the stone floor was magnified by the high ceiling. The crossbow slipped from his hands and skittered away. He lay on his back and watched the werewolf fill the doorway, mouth wide, tongue lolling and glistening like a pink snake.

The creature paused as though appraising the scene, weighing the possibility of a ruse. Oscar used these valuable seconds to lash out with his heavy boot and kicked the door. It slammed shut on the beast, and Oscar jumped up and drove his full weight against it, his goggles finding a deadbolt in the frame. He rammed this home as the creature beat heavily on the door from outside, each blow jarring Oscar, who began a mantra of "Oh shit" over and over again.

The assault on the door suddenly stopped. Rather than relief, Oscar found the silence unnerving as he took in his surroundings. The back wall was made up of a small altar, and a large cross was situated between two chalices. A small pew lay before the altar. On one wall was a bank of square draws; he counted seven of them. He tried not to think about what was inside them, but his mind was playing out his worst nightmares: the drawer opening and Rothschild's long-dead relatives emerging to hold him in a never-ending embrace as mummified faces leered and mocked. He wondered if Georgina might put in a special appearance just for the hell of it.

The thought of his mother-in-law coming back for vengeance made his breath hitch in his throat. He tried to shut it out just like he tried to quell the realization that he was trapped in a place of death, in the dark once the goggles lost their power supply.

It took all of his effort not to scream. But suppressing long-held emotions took their toll, and something gave out as his mind sought out some form of respite from the trauma. So Oscar laughed instead.

And laughed.

And laughed.

Even the pounding on the door as the beast responded to his deranged mirth could not stop him.

Oscar was way beyond it all.

Chapter Seven

Moving away from the console, Ian headed for the exit. En route, he happened to check on the incapacitated guard. The big man remained propped up against the wall. Then Ian realized that there was a small storage cupboard to the guy's left, the door so delicate it butted up against the wall, barely leaving any hint of its existence, save for an indented, beveled edge. What did catch his eye was the tiny stenciled lettering on one corner of the cupboard door.

Weapon Cache.

He went to his knees and pushed the door inward; it bounced free, opening toward him like a shoe draw. Inside, there was a rack housing three side arms—Glock 17s to be precise—plus several magazines.

He pulled the Glocks from their brackets and rammed home the magazines. He ditched the Taser and holstered one of the guns; he tucked another into the waistband of his pants. The remaining weapon he kept in his hand, relishing both the weight and the feel of gun grease against his palm.

With renewed vigor, he went to the exit, checking the corridor both ways before venturing out of the room. His only thought was to rescue the woman who had saved him in more ways that he could count.

Antonia managed to let the bolt fly as the werewolf leaped into the cabin with a savage roar. Surprise and unstable floorboards let her down; the shaft went left rather than center as she stumbled, the bolt, which turned to a silver dash in the light from the porch lamp, pierced the beast's right shoulder. It gave out an unearthly cry that blended great pain and savage anger.

Huge paws smashed into the floorboards at Antonia's feet, sending her toppling backward, the beast's momentum ensuring it slewed into her, rolling over her before its bulk took out the wall separating the lounge from the kitchen.

Pippa cried out in fear and despair when she saw her sister writhing on the floor. Her left arm was a zigzag above the elbow, and her neck had been speared by a shaft of splintered wood. The wound gave out blood in thick crimson pulses.

If Pippa had any doubt her sister was lost, the werewolf made it crystal clear as it emerged through the tattered remains of the kitchen wall. The maw opened wide, eyes jaundiced with hate, and then it brought its jaws together over Antonia's throat, yanking its head upward, dragging her body with it as though it were a plaything. The creature shook the very life out of her as the shaft in the creature's shoulder drew silver figure eights on the air.

With a cry of complete anguish, Pippa tore across the room, the machete held high, the blow already coming down as she got within striking distance. But the wolf was ready, discarding Antonia's remains with a flick of his head, sending it rolling across the cabin floor until it hit a sofa, splashing dark crimson upon the dust sheet.

Pippa aimed for the creature's head, but all she found was a row of vicious teeth. They clamped about her wrist, and the wolf yanked its head to the right. Her arm came off at the shoulder with a sickening pop. Her scream was cut short as talons from the left paw took out her throat.

Her legs gave out, and she fell, glassy eyes staring yet seeing nothing at all. The anger in the beast seemed to dissipate at her passing. A blackened nose sniffed at her body several times before coming to the conclusion there was no further threat.

Then, with an ever-present growl at the back of the throat, it began to feed.

The corridor went on for some sometime before

the featureless walls became a T-junction. There had even been a few moments when Ian contemplated turning back. Fortune had stayed with him, it seemed. There was a small schematic recessed into the wall ahead, indicating The Grange to the east and another area called *The Bunker* to the west.

The temptation to head off toward The Bunker and establish what trove of evidence may be there to indict Rothschild was fleeting, but it was there all the same. Besides, Ian knew that The Grange meant the cinema and that meant he'd be able to get to Alana.

But will you be able to get her out? The thought was there immediately, and it left uncertainty in its wake. There was truth in that he was working in the dark here. The security team was an unknown commodity. More often than not five members of the staff were on duty at any one time. He'd taken one out; there were two in the cinema babysitting Alana. That left two others somewhere in the main building. If Alana's intel and his math were both correct, that was.

The guards he'd seen in the cinema carried side-arms, which was unusual. This was sanction enough to use deadly force once he got into the building. He continued east, and soon the white walls ended at a set of large metal doors. Ian placed his hands upon the cold steel and felt the thrums of an internal locking mechanism.

Serious shit, he thought. Rothschild was pretty keen on keeping prying eyes out of this area. His mind went to The Bunker again. At least he knew the first place he'd be sending the TAC team when he got out of here.

To the left of the doors was a CCTV screen that showed the room on the other side. Ian realized this whole area doubled as some kind of panic room, and from this spot, anyone inside could see the activities of unwanted guests trying to get in.

At that moment, the space beyond the doors looked clear. He waited a few minutes to see if any guards were on a security schedule; when nothing changed on the monitor, he looked at the other controls on the panel below it. There was a red button that had writing etched into it that read SLAM SWITCH. Next to it was a green button that simply said OPEN.

With a final look at the monitor, he hit green and listened to the low click as the locks disengaged. He aimed the Glock into the ever-expanding gap in the doorway, just waiting for a facc to appear so he could put a bullet into it.

Somewhere during his fall down the embankment, Marty had severed his spinal cord. This was, in some ways, a small mercy. He could not feel the pain of his shattered limbs and punctured organs. He could not see anything other than the bright flecks of moonlight dancing on the lake. It was a beautiful sight, and it gave him a sense of peace that he'd not felt for quite some time.

His vision wavered, the image of the lake juddering as his body was dragged a few yards across the rocky shoreline. He knew that the beast that had caught up with him was eating him alive. He should have at least considered the horror of this even if he could not feel it, but he was accepting of it, grateful for it, because he was dying as he had lived, detached from the true pains in his world.

The moonlight appeared to fade, like a lamp on a dimmer switch. He was falling into the darkness of death. And just like the wolf that had buried its muzzle into the hole it had chewed into his abdomen, he relished every single moment.

As he'd exited the steel door in the cellar, Ian had expected to come across security patrols. This had not happened. He'd passed other doors and found only one ajar, and his curiosity had him peering inside.

He found a long bench, and on it were three burgeoning red refuse sacks, tied at the top. He was drawn to them, his analytical mind forever calculating ways to ensnare Rothschild.

Hoping for evidence inside, he carefully unpicked the knot and opened the bag. He saw the piles of clothing—dresses and jeans—before digging deeper and finding personal effects such as a gold bracelet, hallmarked at 18 carats, and a lady's Rolex wristwatch, easily worth ten grand. Not the kind of stuff people would donate. But bangles and wristwatches with traceable serial numbers were ways of identifying individuals you wanted to make disappear. And this piqued his curiosity further. He dug deeper into the belongings and found the passports, two in total.

He recognized them instantly from earlier in the evening; the passports gave their names as Pippa and Antonia Okill, the two game hunters with a penchant for off-the-grid safaris. His earlier suspicions as to why they were here had been given more weight, but the greater mystery was why the Okill's belongings, including their passports, were earmarked for disposal. Last he'd heard, they were living out of Antigua; there was no way could they cross borders without their travel documents. So what was going on? The immediate answer was that perhaps Rothschild didn't expect them to return from the woods. Ian supposed the other bags held the sum contents of the other participants he'd served in the drawing room earlier.

He wanted to check out his theory by looking through the other bags, but time was against him. The security guard in the CCTV room wasn't going to stay unconscious forever. He added another mental note to his TAC team itinerary to retrieve the bags when they raided this place. He re-sealed the bag and left the room to its secrets.

He moved upstairs to the main house, finding it unusually quiet. The corridors had none of the evening bustle associated with entertaining dinner guests. It suggested something else was going on, something that required staff to keep a low profile.

Murder, perhaps?

With this grim thought in mind, he headed for the cinema.

Oscar's night vision goggles sputtered. The inevitability of their failure was now becoming a reality.

In the mausoleum, he had laughed until his throat was raw and his ribs ached. Now he was weeping, the tears trapped in his goggles making them misty. He couldn't take them off, though, because then he would be in total darkness, and there were things in here that flourished in such an environment. Things that were the product of his guilt, from his imagination, corpses that wanted to caress him with skeletal hands and paper-thin skin. His mind was a staunch supporter of this fear and had sold it to him with ease. When he considered the prospect that it was Georgina who was going to be coming for him, fear became psychosis and influence became reality.

The goggles went dark, flooding him with terror before they came back on after a few seconds.

Not much longer, he thought. *Soon I'll be dancing in the dark with my dear old mother-in-law.*

He inhaled through his nose, held it, let it go through pursed lips. He did this several times, an old trick from anxiety management classes he'd attended after his mother died.

He heard a sound—the footsteps of something heavy walking around. At first, horror told him it was coming from inside the mausoleum, but he soon realized it was the beast outside, pacing, stalking him, reminding him he literally was not out of the woods.

The footsteps did, however, seem to be receding, fading with each footfall until he could barely hear it.

It's given up, he thought with renewed hope. *The fucker has lost interest. And when I get out of here, I'm going to skin it alive and wipe my feet on its mangy pelt every fucking day forever.*

He could feel the smile slide across his face as he pushed himself away from the door and turned to face it. He'd give it for as long as the goggles held out; then he'd be able to just ease that door open and get the fuck away from the cursed darkness.

There was a sudden pounding in his ears, his heart sending adrenaline-fueled blood around his body. But he realized with growing unease that the staccato thumping was again beyond the door, and it was *getting louder.* An image flashed through his mind, a bull elephant out at the Samburu National Reserve in Kenya, charging at his jeep in the summer of '95. Yes, a similar sound, a similar pace.

A charge.

Realization came at the very moment his goggles winked out and an impenetrable blackness descended upon him for a few moments.

He had the scream ready, but the door to the mausoleum smashed inward, knocking him off his feet and onto his back, where the wind was blasted out of his lungs. He slid several feet and hit the altar, the cross and chalices tumbling from their perch and clattering around him.

Amid the wreckage of the shattered door, the great wolf considered him for a few moments. Oscar tried to get his lungs to work; he tore off the goggles and could see the beast, its fur tinted by the muted light of the moon outside.

Paws began to move, cautiously at first, talons clicking on the stone floor, kicking aside the machete and crossbow that had been lost to Oscar when the door gave out.

He turned his head away, tears running down his face, the incongruous giggles back on his lips. He couldn't watch the thing come for him, couldn't look at the face that put fetid spittle on his cheeks. He couldn't bring himself to look upon the hideous fangs and great, salivating mouth.

Not that he was afraid of such things; his mind had saved him from that at least. No, the reason he couldn't look into the face of the beast was because he knew without any doubt it would not have the face of a wolf; it would be that of Georgina Cox, cold fingers coming to collect what was owed.

And his penance was destined to be painful.

Chapter Eight

Ian hunkered down with his back to a wall. He'd made it to the theater on the second floor. Above him, there were four paintings that would collectively fetch over forty million pounds on the open market. Sadly, Ian knew these particular works of art had been purchased legitimately, but it certainly gave an indication of the kind of money Rothschild made from his illegal activities.

He peered around the corner and saw the foyer that he knew led to the cinema. It had been fashioned in the design of a theater lobby, scaled down but teeming with authentic touches. There was a popcorn vendor counter, a "Forthcoming Attraction" poster display case that had a white question mark on a black background. The theater doors were roped off with a line of velvet cord between two brass stands. More importantly: there were no guards.

He checked that the way was clear before making for the theater doors, two brown rectangles, each with a darkened portal window. He ducked beneath the velvet cord, dropped to a knee, and nudged open the door to take a look inside.

There was a small carpeted landing; the walls daubed the color of a heady wine. The sloping floor went left, where a corner gave off a muted orange light. Ian followed the contours and risked a quick peek around the corner.

Both security guards from the CCTV had their weapons free and aimed directly at him.

The gunshots and bullets came seconds later, the corner alcove taking several blasts, gouging out plaster and sending clouds of white dust into the small corridor. Ian rolled backward, only his instincts saving him from taking shots to the head.

He didn't get away free, however. Stickiness and heat radiated from the right side of his head, and when he checked his ear with a finger, he found that his lobe was missing.

"Fuckers," he whispered.

There was an oppressive silence following the loud gunshots. Plaster dust drifted in air that reeked of discharged gunpowder.

A gruff voice came from the theater. "Get out here, or the woman dies."

Ian smiled. "Are you going to play nice?"

"Just throw out your gun," the voice said. "Then we'll talk."

They don't have sanction to kill Alana, Ian thought. *Rothschild calls the shots in this place. This is way above their pay grade.*

But they clearly had permission to kill *him*. And he knew they'd try as soon as he stepped from cover.

"What we have here is what they call an impasse," Ian called. "Not sure how we navigate it so we can all walk away without any extra holes."

"I told you the rules," the voice came again. There was something about it; the tone was wrong, as though the person behind the words didn't have his heart in them.

Like he was just going through the motions. *Or providing a distraction.*

An arm clutching a handgun snaked around the corner and let off two haphazard shots before Ian put several bullets into the hand and wrist. The forearm changed shape and wetness splashed the walls. Screaming, the guard staggered into view, his face screwed up with agony, but Ian caught him before he could collapse, spun him around, and shoved him back out into the main theater.

The second guard was firing on his colleague as Ian ducked low and opened his head with a single shot. Both men crumpled without any further sound. Ian hoped the soundproofing would cover the gunfight, but he still moved quickly through the gloom. He found Alana hunkered down between two seats, hands clamped over her ears and her shoulders shivering beneath her raven hair.

He dropped to his haunches and gently placed a hand on her arm, an act that made her cringe and try to retreat further into the aisle.

"Alana, it's me," he whispered. "It's Ian."

"You shouldn't have come here," she said into her hands. "You should've left me."

"That was never going to happen," he said.

She came out from behind her hands; her green eyes were puffy from weeping. She leaned over and hugged him. He took her into his arms, kissed her exposed face over and over.

He muttered into her neck. "One of Rothschild's goons said you had a daughter—Crystal—and she was in danger."

"Crystal was killed five years ago," she whispered into his neck.

"Rothschild?"

"Yes. My ex-husband was a poor customer, ran up debts. My daughter paid for them." Tears came, and Ian felt a burning anger in his chest.

His voice was small. "Why didn't you tell me?"

"I'm telling you now," she said flatly. "My Crystal is gone. But her death will not be in vain."

"This is the reason why you wanted to bring him down." A statement she made no attempt to contest. "We'll get this fucker, Alana. I promise you. Do you believe me?"

She looked up at him with haunted eyes. "I believe you."

He nodded. "Listen, we have to go. Can you use a gun?"

"Yes."

He pulled the Glock from his belt and handed it to

her. He was surprised to see her prime it and click off the safety.

"When we get out of here, you're going to have to tell me where you learned how to do that."

She stood up, determination in her eyes. "No, I don't."

He smiled grimly. "Fair enough."

He went to the guards and took magazines from their belts. *Glocks galore in The Grange*, he mused.

"You okay?" he asked.

"Yeah."

Guns ready, they began their perilous escape.

Through the empty halls and passages Ian and Alana went, the absence of staff making the whole place seem like an abandoned museum. Suits of armor sometimes caught them out as they turned into corridors; the silent sentinels were almost peppered with bullets on three occasions.

Meandering though The Grange for several minutes, they used every alcove and recess for cover. The expectation that a guard would emerge from the shadows and open fire was ever present. But it never happened. Confidence was high as they descended the main staircase into main hall and reception area, its grand chandelier resplendent and a total contrast to the dark mood in the air.

They got to the bottom of the steps, where the

foyer awaited them, and beyond that: the exit.

The security guards came for them as they crossed the hall, stepping out of the drawing room with their batons swinging. Alana put one down, but the second caught her napping; she tripped awkwardly, hitting her head on a pedestal. Ian blasted the guard in the chest, and he went staggering, his knees giving out before he pitched sideways to lie still.

Dazed and moaning in pain, Alana slumped against a nearby wall, knocking a painting askew before crumpling to the tiled floor.

"Alana, come on," Ian said with urgency. "You have to work with me."

She said something, but it was incoherent, a rambling, pain-laced monotone.

Ian made the decision that he was going to have to lift her, but a terrible sound filled the hallway, stopping him in his tracks.

The growling came from the direction of the exit. And with it came ragged breathing. Ian remembered watching a documentary about wild dogs in the Australian outback, the savage snaps and snarls as they fought over moldy carcasses. This sound was just as ferocious and much louder, the high ceilings adding to the soundscape.

When Ian saw the creature crawling into the hall, he held his breath, trying to get hold of his fear. He saw the muzzle and the yellow eyes, the way the gray fur was dark with dried blood. And then he noticed the silver crossbow bolt in the beast's shoulder, the entry wound oozing with a green, purulent substance akin to a toddler's snot.

Realization nuzzled through his fear.

They were hunting you, he thought. *Those guys here tonight were hunting you down like a dog, but it seems you got a start on them. Is that what Rothschild already knew? Is this why there are red bags in the cellar?*

He didn't know the details any more than he knew what the hell this thing was, but he was certain it wasn't in the mood for negotiation. He recognized this as the same creature he'd seen on the CCTV as it suddenly pushed itself up onto its hind legs, magnificent and deadly in equal measure.

Its head tilted back, and the howl it delivered was long and woeful. Ian stood in front of Alana, who was coming to but was still groggy.

Without warning, the beast dropped to all fours and ran at them.

As the werewolf came toward them, Ian lifted the gun. But it was Alana who fired. The shots were loud, bouncing crazily around the hall, an acoustic assault making them both flinch; the tinnitus set in soon after.

The bullets made no impact upon the oncoming juggernaut because it was not the intended target. Instead, Alana took out fixtures of the grand chandelier overhead, and the huge structure fell from the ceiling like a vast teardrop, a trail of dust and chunks of plaster showering down as it landed in the path of the creature.

If the shots were loud, then the detonation of the crystal hitting the hall floor was catastrophic. Both Ian and Alana threw themselves backward, the chandelier exploding like a beautiful bomb, the debris slicing through the air in every direction.

Ian was up on his feet immediately, but Alana was faster despite her recent head wound. They clung together, each frantically seeking out a means of escape as the werewolf rose from the mountain of shattered crystal, its body badly torn and weeping, but the fury of its snarl told them it sought only brutal vengeance.

"Exit is blocked," Ian muttered.

Alana dragged him sideways, alertness now back in her eyes. "We need to go back upstairs."

"We'll be trapped," he said, reluctant to move.

"We go outside, its open ground," she reminded him. "It'll catch us, Ian. We won't stand a chance."

He knew she was right as soon as she said the words. This thing was a predator of the incredible kind. They needed to contain it, limit its abilities.

"Let's go," he said.

They moved in tandem, Ian first, and Alana following, training her Glock in the creature as it tried to find a way through the jagged obstacle separating it from its prey. During this time, the humans ran up the stone steps to the first floor, pausing on the landing and its balcony above to look back and briefly consider if they should shoot the creature from their new vantage point.

The werewolf was already smashing aside the chandelier, the desire to get to them now feeding its fury, making Ian and Alana think better of making a stand.

They fled back down the corridor toward the cinema, the ragged scampering sounds of the beast in hot pursuit following them as it charged headlong after them. They took in air, hot in their throats, lungs burning with exertion, hearts pumping with effort and fear.

Ian risked looking back.

The creature was closing the gap; it was now only several years behind, legs powering it forward despite the cramped space. Ian saw the suit of armor standing proud to his right. As they passed it, he drove his shoulder into the chest plate, smashing the figure into the wall, and it toppled with a clatter of steel seconds later. There was a loud bark, and a thump as something heavy went down onto the carpets, and although temporary, it made Ian feel damn good.

Then he heard the gunshots, and suddenly the walls and bases of the pedestals began to come apart around them. Instinctively, Ian dived to the floor, Alana plowed into a doorway, and the door gave way. She yelped as she fell into the room beyond.

Ian heard bullets whizzing overheard as more automatic fire erupted in the corridor. He caught sight of muzzle flashes twenty yards out; he figured the guy was sporting a semi-automatic rifle; an AR 15 sprang to mind. Even though bullets ripped the air, it was the next sound that garnered all of Ian's attention.

The howl was immediate and ended with a hideous

snort of fury. Despite the gunman down the corridor, Ian rolled onto his back and watched the werewolf as it disentangled itself from the fallen suit of armor. Its advance was slow, deliberate, and impervious to the dangers presented by the sniper. Ian became the focus for its uncompromising yellow eyes, and the growl that came from its muzzle put juddering vibrations in his sternum.

Ian's mind sputtered, was in danger of closing down completely.

Alana's voice was suddenly on the air, sharp and urgent, calling his name shortly before gunshots cut through his malaise. Plumes of blood erupted from the werewolf's pelt, provoking a huge howl of pain. Ian used the distraction and made for the doorway where Alana was hunkered down, gun held high, her left hand supporting her right wrist.

The AR15 barked from down the corridor, causing Ian to cry out in frustration.

"Shoot at the fucking wolfman, you moron!"

"Fuck you, copper," a voice came back, the pronunciation thick and awkward. Ian envisioned the bloated lips of the security guard he'd knocked unconscious outside the CCTV room.

More automatic fire rang out, sporadic and without accuracy as the sight of the incredible creature put a tremor in the shooter's hands.

Ian used the haphazard assault to dive into the room, taking Alana with him. They landed in the gloom on thick carpets. The door was still wide open, and they could see the shadow of the werewolf crawling across the opposite wall, now standing tall as though the man it had once been had not quite given up his true identity.

Scrambling to his knees, Ian shoved the door, sending it slamming it into the jamb with a *thud*, then sprang to his feet as the door suddenly shook in the frame, the creature on the other side pummeling it to gain access.

More shots rang out from behind the door, the sounds dulled by the thick wood.

The werewolf began barking and snarling in a painful rage.

"That guy really doesn't know when to quit," Alana said beside him.

There was a commotion as heavy footfalls and howling came from behind the door. Panicked cries and a single rapport followed, then came a hideous scream, accompanied by a series of squelches and cracking noises.

"We got to get out of this room," Ian said, looking about him. There was a tall window on the right wall. Shelves of books occupied the remaining walls, and a large reading chair and side table sat in the middle of the library.

"Let's get this window open," Ian said as he went to it. Peering out, he could see the gravel drive and open lawns twenty feet below.

"We can't jump." Alana predicted his conclusion before he had a chance to formulate it.

"No," he replied, opening the window and examining the ledge outside. He saw the drainpipe almost immediately. "But we can shimmy down to the ground."

Alana eyed the length of dull lead piping as it descended as a dark vertical line to the gravel driveway below. "Think it'll hold us?"

Ian's eyes looked at her, and his stare was intense as the door behind them took another blow. "If we go one at a time," he said.

Her unblemished brow became a series of crazy ruts as understanding came to her. "Are you insane? I'm not leaving you up here with that thing."

Another loud crash, wood splintered. Pieces of frame flew through the air.

"No time to argue this, Alana," he said, placing a kiss on her furrowed brow. "Please, I'll be down as soon as you're near the bottom of this damn pipe, okay?"

She was reluctant, but fear of the beast smashing its way into the room helped her to see the sense of it all. She climbed onto the window sill, and Ian helped her into position. She clutched the drainpipe and braced off, the small creak coming from the brackets securing the conduit to the wall making her pause until she was sure the whole structure wasn't going to collapse.

Alana began her descent, eyes looking up at him, the pain and terror fusing to make her face appear both ugly and beautiful at the same time. She was ten feet down when the beast beat down the library door, and Ian ducked back into the room to face it.

As the creature entered, the ever-present snarls and growls accompanying it, Ian could hear his lover calling his name over and over again.

Chapter Nine

The creature fell to all fours and stalked Ian through the library. There was a perpetual snarl on its blackened lips, and its elongated facc was a mask of blood-splattered fur. But as it moved, Ian noted that rage had been tempered with caution and when he realized the beast was wary of him, a smattering of hope stoked his resolve.

He raised his gun, aware that it needed a reload. This wasn't the time; the beast would be on him as soon as he tried. He'd tried to count his own shots, figuring he had six left, but it was an estimate at best. With some relief, he remembered he had stowed another weapon in the Taser sheath, and his left hand reached across for it.

The sheath was empty. The gun lost at some point in their skirmishes in the halls and corridors.

How could I have been so reckless?

This thought went through his head in a nanosecond, and if the beast had been making its own calculations as to how dangerous its foe was, it came to a decision to charge a split second later. It closed the distance with a pounce, its body making a whooshing sound as it moved through the dead air.

Ian dived behind the heavy reading chair as the creature landed, swiping it aside with a front paw. The chair bounced across the carpet and smashed into a bookcase; tomes fell from the shelves, their pages flapping like the wings of birds shot from the sky.

In the clamor, Ian rolled left as the chair went in the opposite direction, and the werewolf got confused for a second. Ian used the time to put two shots into its side. The creature recoiled as though branded and created enough space for Ian to escape.

Ian took that chance and sped to the exit, where the door lay in ruins. He scampered over the wreckage and went right, his intention to head for the staircase to the main hall. He powered down the corridor, jumped over the fallen suit of armor, and saw the space open out on to the landing where the stone staircase waited.

But all this time he heard the pounding of the beast racing after him, relentless and with a wrath no man could match. In his mind, he knew that he was buying Alana time to get the hell out of there, though his greatest fear was that she'd be too loyal to leave him behind. He loved and hated her for that in the same moment.

Giving her time to decide was all that mattered, and Ian made a decision that, if it worked, would give them both some space to consolidate their escape. If it didn't, then he would be mere meat in the great beast's gut.

But he had to do something because as he hit the landing he could feel heat on the back of his neck; the fucking creature was almost upon him.

The staircase, flanking twin balconies of fluted stone, dropped off to the main hall. And as soon as he opened the distance between himself and the pursuing beast, Ian dropped to the floor without warning and curled into a ball. He rolled a few feet before he felt the beast hit him, paws beating into his back, winding him as it tripped over his body, legs becoming twisted around each other, its momentum taking the mass of fur onto the balcony, where stone cracked with the force of impact.

The werewolf was a victim of motion as it went over the balcony with a howl of surprise and disappeared to the hallway below.

There was a hefty *thud* but no other sound. Ian rolled over and climbed to his knees. He was tempted to go and look at the damage he'd inflicted, but he needed to get the fuck out of there, and *now*.

There was no way he was getting caught in the main hall, so he jogged back to the library. He scanned ahead and saw the chewed-up body of the security guard spread-eagled at the far end of the corridor. Ian felt nothing for the guy. Serving someone like Rothschild came at a cost.

He went into the library, where the drainpipe waited. He stuck his head out of the window and peered down, his heart lifting as he saw Alana waving desperately to him from the gravel path below.

He tucked the gun into his belt at the small of his back and climbed out onto the windowsill. The cool air was a welcome relief from the stuffiness inside The Grange. Part of him hoped it would somehow rid him of the smell of death that had lodged in his nostrils.

The drainpipe groaned as he began his descent; he even felt the metal give slightly with each movement. He took his time, easing his way down, willing himself not to fall victim to impatience. Luck was still with them, and he didn't want to seem ungrateful.

Without warning, the library window exploded.

A cascade of glass fell onto Ian's head and shoulders, and he felt warmth as shards sliced into the top of his head. Amongst the tinkling din came another familiar growling, which had Ian hugging the drainpipe with his left hand and shoulder and reaching with his free hand for the gun in the small of his back.

He raised his head; the hideous countenance of the werewolf looked back down at him. Its face appeared broken, the body that was trying to scramble out onto the windowsill to grab the drainpipe looked malformed from its fall over the balcony. But it was still determined to kill them all.

"Give me a fucking break, would you?" Ian muttered as he raised the Glock.

He fired three times as the werewolf made an attempt to snag the pipe, the bullets hitting it directly in the face. One of its yellow eyes went out as though someone had turned off a light. The creature immediately slumped, head and one arm hanging over the windowsill.

Ian bowed his head, almost giddy with relief. The great wolf was dead, and they had a fucking chance to get out of there alive. It seemed anticlimactic the way the beast had succumbed, despite how often it had almost ended them.

Based on his own skepticism, he looked up, determined to make sure his assessment wasn't premature. What he saw knocked his mind off-kilter because he didn't see a wolf anymore.

He only saw a man with long, shaggy hair and pale skin. There was an empty socket where an eye should have been, and an arm hung limply against the brickwork. None of this made any real sense, and his psyche made sure he didn't delve too far into thinking about what had just happened. But it was the man's lips that added further incongruity to the whole moment.

They were smiling.

Ian descended the drainpipe and had just made contact with the gravel when Alana grabbed hold of him and smothered him with kisses.

"I thought you were lost to me," she confessed. She held onto him tightly.

"Did you see what happened?" he said.

"Yes."

"How can a wolf be a man?"

"Or a man a wolf?" she added. "My mother used to say all men are beasts underneath."

"You believe that?" he said, looking into her jade

eyes.

"Not anymore," she said, and kissed his cheek.

He nodded and kissed her back. "We need to get clear and get in touch with the TAC team. I think I'm going to have to twist the facts a little at the debrief."

Despite it all, they both smiled.

"Come one," he said, taking her hand.

He intended to cross the lawns and head for the car pool, where an SUV waited with keys stowed under the chassis for emergency extractions. He figured this met the definition, and then some.

A voice came to him, loud and slightly distorted by the Tannoy system projecting it.

"Well, well, DC West and the incorrigible Alana O'Shea," Rothschild said in a mocking tone. "It seems you've got yourselves into a bit of a pickle. To be expected of you, West. If you go sticking your big piggy snout into my business, you will inevitably lose it."

Ian looked about him as though half expecting his tormentor to show himself. "Tell that to your security team. Oh, sorry. I forgot. You've no one left."

"Just like Miss O'Shea," Rothschild sneered. "Husband and child, all gone."

"Fuck you," Alana yelled into the night, face twisted with unbridled rage.

Rothschild chuckled, and the sound wasn't pleasant because it meant that he felt no way intimidated. In fact, he sounded like a man who had the upper hand.

"I think I'm quite safe from your antics," he said. "Quite the little sneak, aren't you, West? Coming to my home and prying into my affairs. Yet it has not helped you tonight, *Detective Constable*."

The last two words came with contempt.

Silence on the Tannoy was supplanted by the breeze whipping across the lawns. The moon remained high, watching everything like a single, bloated eye. Deep in his mind, Ian resisted the connection between the lunar event overhead and the man who was once a wolf.

He used defiance to shut out such thoughts. He turned his anger on Rothschild instead. "I know enough to get a TAC team with a warrant in here on reasonable grounds," he said. "You got an illicit hunt going on here, and your hunters aren't coming back, right? That's just for starters. The warrant is going to throw up plenty of shit to send you to the kind of hell where you belong."

The contempt remained in Rothschild's voice. "Clever little piggy. But why end with telling only half the story? Yes, there's a hunt going on tonight. Yes, people have paid handsomely to be on the guest list. You don't get to succeed in my line of work unless you're prepared to cater to all tastes, all *kinds* of client."

The grounds were suddenly alive with terrible mournful howls, too many to count as they blended on the air. The distant trees were alive with tiny orbs of yellow, dancing in the air like fireflies, but there was a symmetry to them, two sets several yards apart.

They looked like eyes. Many, many eyes.

The roars followed—an aural assault on the senses. Alana gasped when she saw the creatures slink out of the trees, some walking tall, others on all fours.

The pack was wary, of course; one of their own had been taken down by the humans who stood eight hundred yards away. But it added to the thrill of it all, the thrill of the chase.

The thrill of the hunt.

The two humans watched the creatures stalking them. Alana lifted her gun, and Ian followed suit.

"What the hell are we going to do?" she whispered.

He looked at the oncoming wolf pack, their fur white with moonlight, and then back at the drainpipe.

"*Any* idea would be really good right now," she urged.

"Don't I know it," Ian said as he watched the wolf pack tearing across the lawn.

Think, his mind screamed. *For fuck's sake, think.*

He went to one knee, bringing up the Glock to buy them some time. Squeezing the trigger, he took out the lead wolf—a lean male with wiry limbs. The beast's muzzle plowed into the turf, carving a furrow into the lawn. The pack pulled up, guarded.

The largest of the beasts stepped forward and sniffed its fallen comrade, but its malevolent eyes never left Ian. The wolf tipped back its head and unleashed a great, sorrowful howl into the night.

Ian climbed to his feet, the crunch of gravel shockingly loud in the silence left after the howling abruptly ceased. Something in his mind flared, synapses crackling within a maelstrom of thought. The wolves had the advantage over grass, but the oscillating gravel would slow them down long enough to get to—

Where, he questioned. *The house?* No, the pack would be upon them before they got to the drainpipe. He was watching as the wolves began to edge forward. Only the weapon he had trained on them was keeping them reticent.

If he and Alana kept to the driveway skirting around the Hall, it would naturally lead them to the garage, where his SUV waited in the adjoining staff carport. It gave him a token sense of purpose, a sense of hope.

The yellow gravel was their only path to freedom.

We're off to see the wizard, Alana. He suppressed a smile for fear that once it was on his face it would turn into the endless vacant grin of a lost mind.

"The garage," he muttered to Alana. "But stay on the driveway, no matter what."

She was hesitant, actually taking a step backward. "We'll never make it."

Ian reached out his hand, his eyes fixed on hers. "Do you trust me?"

"Yes." No hesitancy this time.

"Then do as I ask. This is our only chance."

Snarls came to them, and they turned to the pack, which was now creeping across the lawn, heads low, black lips bared to reveal long, yellow fangs.

Alana acquiesced with a small nod, eyes bright with fear. Ian gently tugged her arm, and she ceded. They began to move, cautious and ready with their weapons, aware of the pack stalking them on the lawn fifty feet to their left, some hanging back, others creeping forward to try and cut off their retreat.

"Can't allow them to get in front of us," Ian muttered as he quickened his pace, pulling Alana along with him.

The temptation to take down those beasts in danger of intercepting them was a powerful urge that Ian struggled to quell. Their ammo was finite and wasting shots going wide was a risk he wasn't prepared to take unless there was no other option. Sure, the pack was still keeping a respectful distance, the large male—clearly their leader—out in front by a few paces.

A fleeting thought had Ian wondering if the pack would disband if he put the leader down, but there were no guarantees in this game.

With each painstaking step, the two fugitives moved past the main entrance, the steps splashed with dark fluid glistening under the arc lights from the driveway. At the top of the steps was a shredded human torso, too mutilated to determine gender. The fluid oozed from terrible wounds in a series of crimson cataracts.

"Jesus," Ian heard Alana mutter. "This is a nightmare. All of it."

In nightmares you get to wake up, Ian thought grimly. Instead, he said, "The garage is around the next corner, right?"

"Yes."

The edge of the building was twenty yards away, the sandstone walls edged in yellow light. Beyond that, Ian knew the lawn was sculpted to move closer to the manor. This was going to be where they'd have to bolt and take their chances of getting to shelter before the beasts ran them down.

The garage lay ahead, a plain single-story building sitting low and at a right angle to the manor. Accessed by a large rectangular door, Rothschild kept several high-performance cars and two Bentley's in a space that was more akin to a hanger than a garage. Despite its size, it was not the place reserved for staff cars. These were parked beneath the carport fashioned from metal and white canvas, a statement as to their standing in Rothschild's world.

Social etiquette was the least of Ian's concerns. As he and Alana prepared to run, he scanned the carport for his SUV. He could see it parked up next to a white VW Touareg. Ian had a vague memory of the head chef boasting about his new ride.

Ian looked at Alana and whispered, "You ready?"

"No. But we're doing it anyway, right?"

He gave her a weak smile. "No matter what happens, I love you. Never forget that, okay?"

He felt her hand squeeze his tightly.

Ian took a breath and turned to face the wolf pack, which was now ominously close, skulking on the edge of the lawn.

"Let's piss 'em off a little," Ian said as he took aim. The beasts saw him raise the gun and snarled their rage as they scattered. Ian put a bullet in the side of the larger wolf, which yelped as it was hit in the left flank.

"Now, run!" Ian said, and they moved across the driveway, the gravel providing an untrustworthy level of support. Ian slipped after ten yards, rescued only by

Alana shouldering him upright.

They could hear the beasts coming for them. Skittering paws on the uneven ground, growls and hoarse panting prompted thoughts of these savage animals on the move.

Ian hoped he'd done enough. The shot was to rile them, get them whipped up into such a rage they'd tear off in pursuit, regardless of the terrain they had to cross. Indeed, he could hear the scrunch and scratch of grit giving way, the short, sharp yelp of a startled wolf and a dull *thud* of something heavy hitting the harsh ground.

The sound was as satisfying as it was short-lived, giving way to the ferocious growls that appeared to be closer than he felt comfortable. The carport was nearby, only twenty feet away.

Then ten feet and the SUV was now in sight, tantalizingly close.

Their haphazard shadows were cast against the slatted garage doors, freakish shapes illustrating their desperation. Their pursuers were also there, a hem of angular shapes at their monochrome feet.

Ian watched as one shape rising from the shadowy mass splashed on the garage doors. Instinct had him grabbing Alana and forcing her downward.

Both went sprawling, Alana giving out a cry of surprise and pain as the contact with the sharp surface proved unforgiving on exposed palms. A rush of wind passed overhead, the light suddenly blotted by the shape of a leaping wolf. Flipping on his back, Ian put two bullets into its exposed belly, and the animal cried out.

Now maimed, the wolf landed hard and rolled several times before smashing into the garage doors, where it lay broken and still.

Immediately, Ian dragged a dazed Alana to her feet. The pack was closer now, galvanized by the death of another of their order. Snapping, snarling jaws orchestrated their approach, the need to reap vengeance as savage as it was determined.

But Ian sensed something else in the frenetic discord behind him. He felt the excitement oozing from his pursuers. For a split second, he doubted they were going to make it. He shoved the thought away, anger replacing the gap left behind.

Alana was a few paces ahead, and Ian called out to her. "Blue SUV. You go driver's side. Keys are under the front wheel arch."

Before Alana could protest, Ian placed a hand against the small of her back and propelled her forward. Her light frame accelerated across the last few yards, and she slowed herself against the hood of his SUV.

Ian watched her turn, alarm settling in her eyes.

"Get in and fire her up," he yelled as he slowed. "It's the only way you can save my ass."

He saw the recognition of the facts, such as they were, put determination in her movements. He watched her move fast to the SUV, following his hasty instructions.

He spun around, gun ready to face the pack, which by this time was a mere ten meters away. Despite their bloodlust, they pulled up as they saw him take aim. The surface beneath their paws betrayed them, and their gait was clumsy.

Ian did not hesitate; he shot one smaller wolf in the face, sending a yelp and many teeth into the night. The pack made for him as one, led by the huge male that was now hell-bent on getting its teeth into him.

The gun spat more rounds; two more unnatural creatures were removed from this natural world. Ian was frustrated that other pack members seemed to get in the way each time he tried to take out the leader. Then he realized it was deliberate, a sacrifice for a feral greater good.

It was in these moments of realization that Ian finally felt fear. His legs locked up, his belly felt as though it was filled with iced water. The Glock was suddenly heavy and unstable in his grasp.

He pulled the trigger, and the gun clicked. *Empty*, he thought. *Out of bullets and out of luck, fella.*

The pack leader howled, and his entourage padded to a stop. There was something in the great beast's demeanor as it paced back and forth, its eyes never leaving his, and Ian recognized immediately what it was.

It was the guise of victor of the vanquished. This magnificent, terrible creature was relishing the moment before the kill, champion of its world of darkness. Ian decided in those seconds that there existed far greater evils than the likes of Rothschild.

Oddly, Ian's mind was suddenly at peace, and he prepared for the onslaught. Yes, it would be bright agony, but he hoped such things would be fleeting. At least Alana would live. That was all that mattered now, after all.

The great beast stepped closer, still wary of him. Its tongue, a slab of glistening pink and gray mottled flesh, hung like a curtain, tendrils of saliva spattering the gravel. Then there were the eyes, the cold light of malice manifesting in its unrelenting gaze. Once more the wolf raised its head to the sky, its black lips pursing.

But instead of the mournful howl came the huge growl of a car engine, and suddenly the whole scene was awash with headlights on high beam. Blinded, the wolves withdrew several paces, the big male barking in pain and fury that once more it was in danger of having its feral needs thwarted.

The headlights intensified as the SUV emerged from the carport, the crunch of gravel still loud in the chaos. To Ian, it was the flood of hope he needed to get his legs moving. He stepped to one side, and the vehicle pulled up beside him. He threw away the empty gun as he yanked open the front passenger door and jumped into his seat.

"Get us the hell out of here," he gasped.

"With pleasure," Alana smiled.

But as he closed the door, the huge head of the male wolf wedged itself in the doorframe, its snapping jaws frenzied and wanton. Ian cried out in horror, and Alana's scream was shrill within the confines of the cab.

Ian turned in his seat, forcing his knees under the wolf's maw. With his free hand, he pushed the head against the door as he pulled it toward him, trying to inflict enough pain to make the vicious animal pull back.

The car lurched forward, Alana engaging the shift to displace the beast. For a brief moment, the wolf seemed to be holding the car in place; Ian gritted his teeth as he yanked the door closed on the coarse fur of the beast's throat. Then the SUV was moving, the creature dragging along with it, the spray of gravel hitting the garage doors like hail on a tin roof.

Rather than lose its resolve, the werewolf increased its efforts to gain purchase. With renewed vigor, it shook its head, breaking free of Ian's grasp as its front paws gained purchase by digging its claws into the vehicle's frame with the awful squeal of metal. It hauled itself further into the doorway, its muscular torso emerging from the dark. Taking advantage of its new position, the beast began to heave its body forward.

Jaws came down, and Ian instinctively jerked his arm back before teeth snapped shut on empty air. Another wolf smashed into the side of the vehicle, rocking the SUV; a starburst of cracks appeared in the rear window. The car was moving now, but the weight of the creature trying to crawl into the vehicle made it lean to the left. Not yet strapped in, Ian found himself sliding from the seat. He relinquished his grip on the beast and grabbed the back of the seat as he brought up a foot and braced it against the wolf's chest, then pushed with everything he had.

"Move your feet!" Alana's voice was loud and etched with fear. Ian found a Glock by the side of his head.

"Slide backward," she yelled. He slithered back against the dashboard, the gear shift digging into his thigh, his head pressed at an angle to the windshield.

The gun was loud, the muzzle-flash like lightning striking the cab. The wolf yelped as the bullet tore off its left ear; the beast tried to pull away from the gun and tumbled away from the vehicle.

Ears ringing, Ian sat upright and yanked the door shut as Alana worked through the gears. He looked into his wing mirror; the wolves were continuing the pursuit but had become small shapes on the landscape, the building behind them remaining an irrepressible image.

Ahead, the great gates provided a skeletal barrier but, given the temerity of their endeavors, Ian and Alana raced forward, regardless. Ground fog swirled about the pillars to either side of the gateway and was given an eerie luminescence by the SUV's harsh headlights. High hedges flanked either side of the railings, and it was from one of these that a figure emerged to stand steadfast, a raised shotgun aimed at them.

Ian recognized the arrogant swagger of Rothschild a few seconds before he realized Alana was slowing their vehicle. He looked across at her, but she was staring out through the windshield, her mouth pulled taut with hate.

"We can't stop," Ian urged. "Not now. We have to go through that fucker if needs be."

Ignoring him, Alana dropped her window, the hum of the motor bringing a sense of normality to their situation. With the car continuing onward, Ian watched as Alana leaned out of the cab, one hand on the wheel, the other clutching the Glock.

It's a statement, Ian thought. *Yeah, she could just run the fucker down, but she wants some control, she wants to end him her own way. For her daughter, if not for herself.*

Alana let off two shots that had Rothschild going down on one knee. The shotgun discharged seconds later, and Ian's wing mirror disintegrated, taking out his window in the process and peppering him with glass.

Alana stamped on the accelerator, and the SUV closed the distance fast. Credit to Rothschild, he almost clambered out of the way, but Ian could see their malicious host had been caught by one of Alana's bullets and it impeded his escape enough for the SUV's front quarter to clip him and send his body spinning into the bushes.

The vehicle took out the gates seconds later, smashing them off of their hinges and toppling a pillar in the process. The front fender was ripped off in the collision, and the hood rose like an inverted "V" at the center, and they'd lost a headlight. Despite this, the vehicle sped off, neither of its occupants prepared to look back.

In the bushes, Rothschild lay on his back in quiet agony. Both his legs were broken, one of them had a gunshot wound to the thigh. His body shivered as he looked to the night sky. For a moment he fancied he'd seen a shooting star, but there were no wishes to be made; his mind was too fogged to consider it.

Through this haze, Rothschild could hear the growling. He lifted his head to see the great wolf approaching, its image wavering as his eyes fought to focus.

"If this is about a refund, you should've read the small print." He chuckled.

The beast now stood over him, eyes fierce and without mercy.

Rothschild could feel the blood pumping from his thigh. The bullet had shredded his femoral artery and time was no longer a friend.

"You realize you're missing an ear, I assume?" he said thickly before his head flopped back onto the wet grass. Death took him seconds later.

The great beast sniffed at the fresh corpse and turned away. The remnants of his pack trotted up to him, their keen eyes waiting for their leader to command them.

After several seconds, he gave out a sharp bark and padded back down the driveway toward the hall and the woodlands beyond. His dutiful comrades followed without sound.

When Alana was sure they were no longer being followed, she stopped the SUV in the middle of the road.

"What now?" she said.

"We call it in."

She placed a hand on his thigh, and Ian reached down for it, the contact reconnecting him to some kind of reality.

"Think they'll believe us?" she whispered.

"Would you?"
Her silence told him everything he needed to know.

ABOUT THE AUTHOR

Dave Jeffery is author of 14 novels, two collections, and numerous short stories. His *Necropolis Rising* series and yeti adventure *Frostbite* have both featured on the Amazon #1 bestseller list. His YA work features critically acclaimed *Beatrice Beecham* supernatural mystery series and *Finding Jericho*, a contemporary mental health novel that was featured on the BBC Health and the Independent Schools Entrance Examination Board's recommended reading lists.

Jeffery is a member of the Society of Authors, British Fantasy Society (where he is a regular book reviewer), and the Horror Writers Association. He is also a registered mental health professional with a BSc (Hons) in Mental Health Studies and a Master of Science Degree in Health Studies. Jeffery is married with two children and lives in Worcestershire, UK.

ABOUT THE AUTHOR

And be sure to check out these other novellas from

Grinning Skull Press

"Neil Davies weaves Norse mythology and modern horror into a stunning tapestry of terror. You will never again enjoy the quiet of your own house."

– Tom Deady, Bram Stoker Award winning author of HAVEN and WEEKEND GETAWAY

THE DEMON GUARDIAN

Neil Davies

CHAPTER ONE

It was one of those rare mornings when Dennis Parkes woke at peace. Cautiously, he lifted his head, waiting for the quick, shadowy movements seen from the corner of his eye, the sibilant whispering filling the stale air of the small bedroom. There was nothing. Just still, silent darkness.

He thought of waking his wife, Swan, to share his sense of relief and happiness, but she had never heard the voices or seen the shadows move. If he woke her, she would be angry at being disturbed more than an hour before the alarm was due. It would ruin his mood. It would ruin the stillness. He eased his head back onto the pillow and lay awake, enjoying the silence, the peace.

Slowly, dawn lit up the window through the thin curtains, and birdsong twittered and whistled through the trees of nearby Ottmor Wood. If only all mornings could be like this, he would not need the medication, the therapy. It might even make his life with Swan less combative.

If only.

Wyatt Road lay quiet and sleepy on the outskirts of Anbal, a small village on the Wirral Peninsula. The commuter traffic, from Liverpool to the north and Chester to the south, bypassed Anbal on the M53 motorway. What little diverted through the narrow main street of the village itself passed the end of Wyatt Road without any thought of turning in. Wyatt Road was a dead-end. If you didn't live there and were not visiting, your only destination would be the turning circle just before the wooden stile leading to Ottmor Wood.

It was the quiet, more than anything, that had drawn Swanhild Parkes to number 20 when it came up for sale. A narrow mid-terraced house, it stood more or less equidistant between the end of the road and the wood. Built in the early 1930s, it had more-recent additions of a concrete driveway at the front, newly installed plumbing and electrics, and a narrow, but long, well-groomed garden at the back. That was eleven years ago, when she had persuaded Dennis that this should be their first family home. Now, standing at the kitchen sink, staring at the overgrown lawn, the legs of upturned plastic chairs like skeletal limbs reaching up from the long grass, she felt nothing but despair.

"It's not my fault I got made redundant," shouted

Dennis from somewhere behind her. She had almost forgotten they were mid-argument. The same argument they had had almost weekly for the last three years.

"No," she said, agreeing. "But it is your fault that the grass hasn't been cut for weeks."

"You know it hurts my back."

"We can't afford to get someone in anymore," she said, striving to be both truthful and understanding. "Since you can't do it, *I'll* have to do it at the weekend."

"I'll worry if you do that. I don't want you to do that."

His voice almost whined. She hated it when he whined.

"Yes, well, there's not much choice, is there?" She turned from the sink to face her husband. "Now, I have to get to work."

"I'll move the car," said Dennis. "May as well go to the shop while I'm out."

He turned and began burrowing through the accumulated clutter under the stairs for his shoes.

Swan wanted to be even more truthful. She wanted to tell her husband that he was a morbidly obese, out-of-work man in his early forties, and that it was no wonder his back and joints hurt, given the weight they were carrying. But she knew the redundancy had hurt him badly, destroyed his confidence, shoved him into depression, and that the weight gain was almost completely due to emotional eating since then. He was not currently fit for work, mentally or physically. She wanted to tell him these things, but she knew it would just deepen his depression and worsen an already terrible self-image. He needed to know she supported him, still loved him, despite all that had happened.

Dennis had found his shoes and, with some difficulty, put them on. Breathing heavily, he led the way out of the front door. Swan shrugged on her one and only coat and followed.

Dennis reversed his old Peugeot 405 out of the narrow driveway and waited, the engine idling. He felt comfortable in the car, able to relax, away from whispered voices, away from Swan. Alone. It had been bought for the long drive to his last place of work, and he held on to it stubbornly after the redundancy. Big and impractical it might be, given how little driving he now did, but it was *his*. And it was the only thing that connected him to his old life. His purposeful, *employed* life. When he hadn't felt quite so worthless. When he didn't spend days in introspection and deepening depresssion. When he felt confident his wife loved him.

Swan's Vauxhall Corsa reversed out, and the bright pink of the bodywork pulled a slight smile out of his frown. Even she agreed she bought it more for the colour than the car itself.

They waved to each other as she drove off, and Dennis waited until he saw her safely negotiate the junction at the end of the road before he put the Peugeot into gear and headed for the shops.

Just get the essentials and back home.

But did he really want to be home? There was nothing there but an empty house, another long day of watching the clock ticking slowly by, the flash of movement from the corner of his eye—and the voices.

He wanted to tell Swan, he really did. But how do you tell your wife that you hear voices in the home you share? She already thought him fat and useless, blamed him for his depression and for failing to get another job. To admit to hearing voices and seeing things would finally convince her he was completely insane. She would probably leave. He couldn't risk that.

Only two other people knew about the voices and the shadows: his local general practitioner, Dr. Banks, and his one and only friend, Travis Newman. The only two people he had told differed in their reactions.

"It's not that unusual," Dr. Banks had said. "Particularly in someone suffering from clinical depression, like yourself."

"But what do the voices mean?" said Dennis. "Why are they mostly unintelligible? Shouldn't they be sending me messages from God or something?"

Dr. Banks smiled. "The mind is a complex thing," he said. "It can push bad and unpleasant thoughts aside if it doesn't want to deal with them. It separates them, and they become a different part of you."

"You mean like another person in my head?"

"Not quite, but another aspect of you, certainly." Dr. Banks removed his narrow-framed glasses and held them in his right hand, twisting them back and forth as he spoke. "These are things you don't want to have to cope with just now, so they're pushed into the background. And mostly, that's where they stay. But every now and then they push back, and that's where the voices are coming from."

"So it's all in my mind," said Dennis. "Does this mean I'm psychotic or something?"

Dr. Banks shook his head. "No. It's not any kind of psychosis. It's *dissociation.* Like I said, it's quite common among those suffering from depression."

Travis, on the other hand, saw things slightly differently.

"So, you hear voices. Are they always in your head, or sometimes from outside?"

They had been sitting in their local Sainsburys cafe, meeting up during Travis's lunch break from his nearby office job, and before Dennis went shopping. Talking with Travis boosted Dennis's self-confidence enough to make it round the aisles without panicking.

"Sometimes in my head, sometimes not," said Dennis, keeping his voice low. He was sure some of the old people at neighbouring tables were listening.

"I don't reckon it's anything to do with depression," said Travis, casually dismissing what Dennis had told him about the doctor's opinion. "I think it's a lot simpler than all that stuff."

"Oh yes?" said Dennis, doubtfully. As a general rule, he sided with doctors over laymen, but he always had time for Travis's thoughts on matters, however outrageous they might turn out to be. "And so what do you think it is?"

"Simple." Travis leaned closer, lowering his voice to a whisper. "Your house is *haunted*."

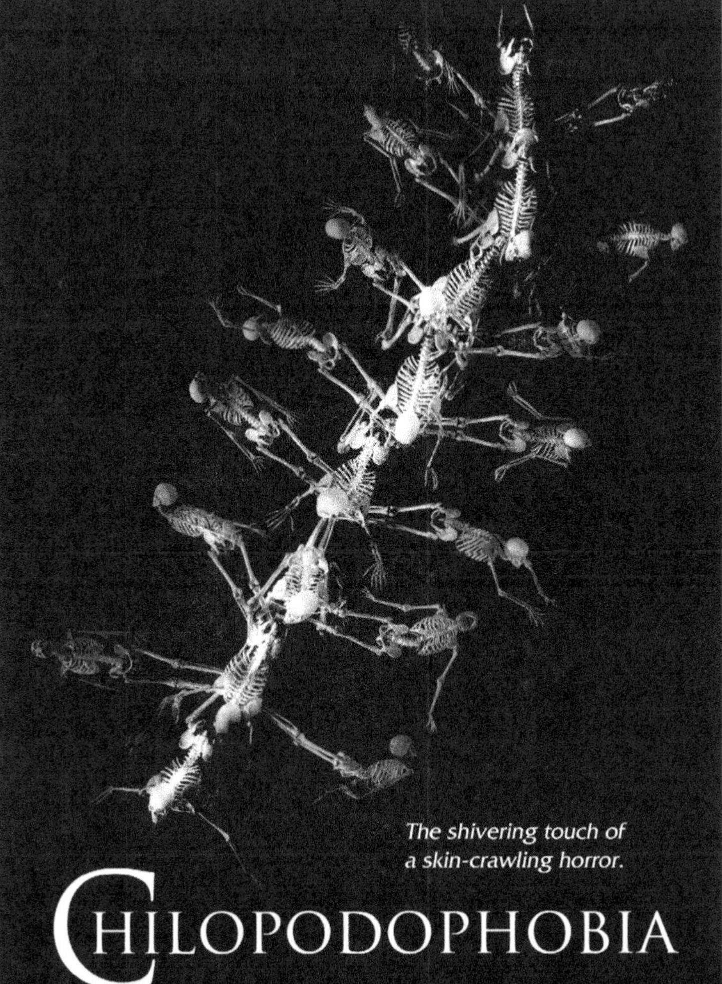
The shivering touch of
a skin-crawling horror.
CHILOPODOPHOBIA
Paul McMahon

Cady entered the house when Uncle Fritch gestured him through the door. Ezzy waited for him at the end of a short hallway. He walked after her, hurrying as she turned right. A doorway to the kitchen stood on the left after he took the turn; he caught a glimpse of an older woman in an apron cooking something that smelled terrific. Ezzy walked past, then took another right. Cady followed and stepped into a large foyer.

He bit his tongue before he could say a word. The wallpaper in here was a dark maroon with an ugly black swirl pattern that swallowed the light. He kept walking, noting the large staircase leading to the second floor and the smallish door beneath it, probably leading to a cellar. He saw a crack in the wall running from the cellar door to the skirt board, and one of the balusters was missing halfway up. The carpet here was dark red and frayed in places along the wall, the woodwork darkly stained. A huge chandelier caught his attention. Only a few candle flame-shaped bulbs shone. Even if every one of the dozens of light bulbs was lit, Cady thought it would still be gloomy in here.

Ezzy turned left through a doorway. Cady glanced

behind him for Uncle Fritch, but he must have gone into the kitchen. He recognized the inside of the front door, mostly because the stone turret stood beside it. The decorative hinges weren't present on this side. A small, arched opening in the turret revealed the start of the spiral staircase Ezzy had told him about.

He walked after her and entered an average-looking study, dark wood and deep red leathers, maroon curtains and brass fittings. A small home bar stood on the left side of the room, but books were lined up on top, where there should be bottles. On the right, the twin windows he'd seen from outside. In front of them sat a worn green couch, its color out of place, angled away from the window and out into the room. Behind it, a tall reading lamp spotlighted the end of the couch. A medical journal was tented on a pillow. Uncle Fritch must have been reading when they'd pulled in.

"This is it," Ezzy said, turning around and leaning against the huge fireplace on the far wall. "Home sweet home."

"Impressive inside and out," Cady said.

"I thought you'd like it."

He took a step toward her, wanting to embrace her just once more before they slipped under Uncle Fritch's more prudish rule, but before he got close, the man cleared his throat from the doorway behind him.

"Ezzy," Fritch said. "Grace is getting dinner ready. Would you be so kind?"

"Of course, Uncle."

Ezzy brushed Cady's shoulder as she headed back

the way they'd come. He watched her go, then spotted Fritch watching him, probably convinced he was staring at her ass. He forced a smile for the old man.

"This'll give us a little time to talk man-to-man," Uncle Fritch said. He glanced into the foyer, then scurried to the bar and reached underneath it. Before Cady could announce that he didn't drink, Uncle Fritch lifted a clear pitcher filled with something pink to the bar.

"Ezzy told me you don't drink," he said. "So I mixed this old family recipe up just for you. It's iced tea sweetened with watermelon. Sounds like a kid's drink, I know, but I guarantee you've never had anything like it."

"Sure, I'll try it," he said. Uncle Fritch dumped ice in a highball glass and then filled it with pink. He pushed Cady's drink across the bar, then dumped two ice cubes into another rocks glass and turned to the bookshelf behind him. "Ezzy's a militant teetotaler," he said. He slid a thick volume of poetry aside and pulled out a bottle of Dewar's Scratched Cask Scotch Whiskey. He splashed two fingers into the glass, downed it, and then poured one finger in its place.

Cady closed his mouth and swallowed.

Fritch tucked the bottle away and replaced the book in front of it. "Between you and me, okay?"

Cady nodded and saluted with his glass of watermelon tea. He rested on the arm of the green sofa. The way it was angled made him want to shove it back against the wall. A quick glance revealed substantial water damage to the window behind it. What he could see of the wall was badly discolored, too.

Fritch settled into the large leather rocking chair across the coffee table from him. He took a deep swallow of his Scotch Whiskey, shut his eyes for a few seconds, and sighed.

Cady sulked at his glass of pink tea.

"Ezzy's told me not to lead with subjects that get my dander up," he said. "Doesn't leave us much to talk about, so I guess it's up to you."

He leveled his gaze directly at Cady and waited. Cady took a slow breath and sipped his drink. The sweetness hit him hard, cloying in its intensity. He swallowed and managed to keep most of the reaction off his face. "This is pretty good, once you get past the sweet," he said.

"It was Ezzy's favorite growing up."

Cady swirled his drink, surprised there were no bits of fruit in it. He took another sip, and this time, prepared for the onslaught, he liked it even more.

"So what do you do with yourself, Cady," Uncle Fritch asked.

"Between jobs, currently, the economy trashed as it is."

Fritch smiled. "The state of the economy is one of those things Ezzy won't let me talk about." The man took a slow swig, as if to rinse away his opinions, then returned his attention to Cady. "What would you be doing if the economy hadn't left you jobless?"

"Retail work, I suppose. Salesman-type stuff. Not that I'm very good at it."

Fritch creased his brow. "If you're not good at it,

why would you choose it?"

"It's easy to do, and it brings in enough money to get by so I can concentrate on my real work, which is playwriting."

Fritch's eyebrows went up. "Playwriting? Unusual. Most people would just say 'writing' and leave it at that."

Cady nodded. "I've done that in the past, but the word encompasses so much it's always followed by the question 'What kind of writing?' which drags a conversation out."

"You don't like long conversations?"

Cady shrugged. "A playwright will live or die by the strength of his dialogue. How could I convince you I was any good if my answer prompted a usual or predictable response?"

Fritch thought for a moment. "What am I going to say next?"

"You're going to ask me if I've written anything you've heard of."

"Exactly what I was thinking."

"I've haven't had anything produced, yet, no."

"Interesting phrasing," Fritch said.

Cady took another sip of his drink. If he wasn't careful, Fritch could start asking about his past, which would not do at all.

"Are you close to your family? Do they live around here?"

"Not especially. I betrayed their expectation that I follow in the family business."

"What business?"

Cady swallowed. Was it his imagination, or was something squiggling beneath Uncle Fritch's collar?

"Furniture," Cady said. "Unfinished."

Fritch downed the last of his drink and stood. He wandered behind the bar again, pausing to run a finger along the spine of the poetry book, and then dumped his ice into the sink with a *clunk*. He reached under the bar and stood with a can of diet soda.

"You shunned your family's retail business so you could work in other people's retail shops?"

"Thus, the nature of their annoyance with me."

Cady downed his own drink and stepped toward the bar. Kid's drink or not, he'd acclimated quickly. His mouth watered while Fritch refilled his glass. When he took it back, it was all he could do not to gulp it down like a man wandering out of the desert.

"Ah, Grace," Fritch said.

Cady turned to see the older woman from the kitchen standing in the doorway. She wrung her hands together just beneath her breasts. Her skin was so pale her hands almost disappeared in front of her white apron.

"Pardon, sir," she said. "Dinner is served."

"Beautiful," Uncle Fritch said. He poured his soda into a glass, then gestured to Cady's drink. "Refill?"

Cady gaped at the empty glass in his hand. It had just been full. When had he done that? In a daze, he handed the glass to Uncle Fritch. His gaze locked onto the edge of the big man's collar. He could have sworn something moved under there.

Lake Livingston: August, 1961

Mark Gaitlin is 15, the son of one of the wealthiest men in Texas, and on the most boring summer vacation of his life. His days are filled with the pomp and circumstance of country club life, while his nights are a parade of one embarrassment after another at the hands of giggling teenage girls.

But the piney woods above Lake Livingston are dark at night, and they hold many secrets for an impressionable youngster on the cusp of becoming a man. And one night, after skinny dipping in the lake with a mysterious local girl, Mark Gaitlin's life takes a crazy turn into the fire and brimstone religion of backwoods snake handlers and abandoned villages haunted by old family secrets. If he can survive the snakes and the ghosts and his own family's dark history, he just might make it out of the woods alive.

And something else…he just might become a man.

Death awaits you. Tim Ritter has just a few months left. At least that's what the doctors have told him.

But then he's been offered a second chance at life – and love. For a price. But is the price too high? The sacrifice too great?

Find out one man's answer to those questions in Dan Foley's Gypsy, now available in print and for Kindle, Nook, and Kobo e-readers.

www.ingramcontent.com/pod-product-compliance
Lightning Source LLC
Chambersburg PA
CBHW070458170726
48291CB00008B/2558

* 9 7 8 1 9 4 7 2 2 7 3 1 6 *